History can be haunting.

URBAN

LEGENDS

OF

LINCOLN

COUNTY

MISSOURI

NORMAN MCFADDEN

Urban Legends of Lincoln County Missouri

Norman McFadden

URBAN LEGENDS OF LINCOLN COUNTY MISSOURI

POLSTON HOUSE

NORMAN MCFADDEN

Published by Polston House Publishing LLC
www.Polstonhouse.com

Published in the United States of America

Contents

Dedication

You know they say that behind every good man there's a better woman. In my writing career there are actually two great women. I started writing later in life because of a reading and spelling problem that I had. It was seven years ago, and I was in my sixties. I moved into the senior resident apartments in Troy, Missouri.

It was there that I met Miss Jane Lackett. I didn't realize it at the time, but that day was going to change my whole life. Me and Jane got to talking and I told her that I had stories in my head that were driving me crazy! And that I needed to put them on paper.

However I didn't have the knowledge to do it. She explained to me that she was a tutor and she had helped people with their reading and writing. so I asked her if she be interested in helping me? And she agreed.

Let me tell you a little bit about Miss Jane. She spent 20 years in the service until she could retire with a pension. After retiring she joined the grandparents Club at the school to help kids. Miss Jane, I salute you because without your help, My two books and writing for the Lincoln County Journal for 2 years, and now my third book would not have been possible! Thank you Miss Jane Lackett!

Now for the other lady that helped me with my writing career. This dedication goes out to Miryah Polston. She is the lady that takes my chicken scratches and makes them sensible for you to read! A wonderful job she does, and she is my Editor. She was the Editor for my first two

7

books, she edited every story that was sent in to the Lincoln County Journal for the last 2 years and now she has helped me to edit this book!

Thank you Miryah Polston! These two ladies are wonderful ladies and I salute both of them. Without you two this would not be possible. Thank you both from the bottom of my heart and God bless.

- Norman McFadden

1

THE SCREAMING CHIMNEY

On September 30th of 1816 a precious baby boy named Simeon Thornhill was born. He was raised by humble God-fearing parents in a small house in rural Kentucky. As a young boy Simeon set his heart on going to California and striking it rich in the gold mines. Once he had become a man he set off to find his fortune. He was gone for many years before coming back to the Mid-West. When he returned it was with a beautiful wife and enough gold to have sunk a battleship (or so they say).

Simeon and his wife bought a large chunk of land and settled right here in Lincoln County, Mo. Right on a little road that you might know, about two miles outside of Troy lies Thornhill Cemetery Road. The chimney of the old homestead still stands a short distance from the cemetery to this very day. But back to our story.

Simeon was quite proud of his wealth and liked to make sure that everyone knew it. So one of the first thing that he did was purchase some slaves. As time passed Simeon came to like one of the slaves very much and they became good friends. This slave, named Giles was more like a companion than an actual slave. Oftentimes Friday and Saturday nights you would find the two drinking together and playing cards.

Things were good until the Christmas Eve of 1858. On this particular evening things had been going well, if not a bit on the quiet side. The two men decided to step outside for a smoke as they continued to chat and drink. It was then that Simeon said something that Giles did not like, so Giles responded by saying something Simeon did not like.. The strangest thing then happened, Giles walked over to his friend and slapped him right across the face. Simeon did not return the blow, but in his shock immediately turned and left the man that he thought was his friend.

Later that evening after Simeon had fallen asleep for the night a loud racket awoke him. He listened to the sound of Giles ranting and hollering outside. Then the man went to banging on the front door saying that he needed to talk to Simeon. His wife held onto his arm and pleaded with him not to go to the door. But Simeon just insisted that he had to see what was going on down there. And with that he headed down the stairs and out of the house.

Right as Simeon stepped across the thresh hold Giles charged him with a huge knife, repeatedly stabbing Simeon in the belly, then he rushed off into the night. Simeon Thornhill lay dying in a puddle of blood on his own front door step.

His wife hearing the commotion ran down the stairs just in time to witness the man disappear in the darkness as her husband lay clinging to life at her feet. She dropped to the floor and cradled her beloved in her lap as she wept. All of a sudden she let out a wail so loud, so full of all her grief that it echoed through the huge home's massive stone chimney and was heard throughout the countryside. Some folks even said that they had heard the haunting wail all the way in Troy.

Simeon clung to life for five days when he finally succumbed to his injuries on December 29th of 1858 at the age of 42. After the attack, Giles was quickly found and arrested. They had been keeping him at the Troy jail awaiting his punishment. On New Year's Day of 1859 some friends and family members of Simeon Thornhill gathered outside of the jailhouse. It was evident that they had determined to make an example of Giles. The party of several dozen men overtook the jail and gained entry. They found the keys and took Giles out with them. Where exactly they took the man is highly debated, but it is told that they nailed him to a stake and burned him alive.

These are our Lincoln County ancestors, and Simeon and Giles are both buried in the Thornhill Cemetery.

Now I spoke with a man that lives right near the chimney, and these are his words. "There are strange things happening in my house that I cannot explain. I hear footsteps in my room when I am trying to sleep, and when I am watching TV I often see shadows moving from room to room."

There are also many witnesses who say that they have personally heard the chimney wailing in it's grief as if it remembers the past tragedies of that fateful night. They say it screams the loudest on a moonlit winter's evening as the wind courses through the trees. Maybe it's just the wind some say, but then again maybe it's not.

Romans 12:19"Dearly beloved, avenge not yourselves, but rather give place unto wrath: for it is written, Vengeance is mine; I will repay, saith the Lord."

2

ELSBERRY CAVES

The little town of Elsberry, Missouri has many buried secrets, and this reporter dug one up about the caves right outside of town. Folks around here say that they are used by Satan worshipers in the middle of the deepest darkest nights.

I had to follow my instincts on this lead and headed straight to the streets of quiet Elsberry for more information. I set my sights on the grocery store and stationed myself right out front asking everyone who passed about the caves outside of town. While there were people who had no idea what I was talking about, there were others who all but ran away from me when I mentioned the caves. Well that certainly got me to thinking, and wondering what in God's name was out there?

Finally I had some luck. A little old lady, easily in her seventies, stopped and said that she would tell me what she knew about the caves. But she warned me that if this was for an article not to mention her name. She explained to me that those involved are everywhere and that she would fear retaliation if they knew who it was that had said these things. She had lived in this town for over thirty years and they would instantly know who she was. I easily promised as I do not want her to suffer for speaking the truth.

She wasn't sure what the crews had been drilling in the caves for, but one day they hit a steam pocket, or so they said. But it was practically the next day when they came back and moved all their equipment and never drilled there again. In her honest opinion those drilling crews had drilled straight into 'The Gates of Hell' and released the Devil himself right into the town of Elsberry. She told me that if she had the money that she would move away this very day. And with that she turned and walked away.

Now my head was spinning in circles, I just knew that there had to be more for me to find out than just this tiny bit of information. I knew I wasn't going to get any further where I was at, so I moved over to the VFW hall. I hoped to have some luck there since most veterans aren't scared of a few Satan worshipers.

It was here that I met another lady who was willing to talk, but also did not want her name mentioned. She was a tiny lady with gray hair who hunched over her homemade cane as she walked. I stood mystified as she told me her horrifying tale.

"I moved here about forty years ago, I was in my thirties then. There was a lot of talk about witches, warlocks and devil worshipers but I paid it no nevermind. But one of my friends told me that if I didn't believe it to go on out to the caves where they meet on Friday nights. Well, we all know that curiosity killed the cat, so I just couldn't keep myself at home that Friday night. I got my camera and headed right out there to see for myself what I could see."

"I got there and there were cars everywhere, it looked like they were having a big 'ol family reunion right out there. I parked and headed to the cave itself and was shocked at the size of it. It was more than big enough to drive into. There was a great big bonfire and people were all around it. Most of the people were dressed up in hooded white robes and talking in weird tongues and I thought they were all crazy."

"In the back of the cave was a man standing on a wooden bench, he was dressed in an all black robe with a hood that covered his head. I guess he was their leader because he was the only one in black. He stood there petting the prettiest fluffy white cat I had ever seen."

"I was sneaking taking pictures, but with the flash off because I didn't want to get caught. I watched as the man in the black robe held the cat high up in the air, suddenly everybody started yelling and hollering and making all sorts of noise. I guessed that the cat was their guest of honor at this party. It didn't take me long to figure out why. The man took the cat and laid it on the bench and pulled out a big knife. He did things to that cat that even now I don't feel comfortable talking about it."

"I took a lot of pictures that night before I headed on my way home. I thought that no one had even noticed me, but strange things began to happen. No even one of the pictures that I took developed. But the worst of it was that very week my youngest daughter, Patricia passed away. The doctors said that there was no reason for it, there was no cause."

The woman pulled a handkerchief from her purse and wiped her eyes, cleared her throat and spoke again. "But I know why my little Patricia died, those people out there in the caves put a curse on me." She let the tears run down her cheeks now. "And that is why you cannot mention my name." She told me bye and walked away.

With her story in my head I headed on out to the caves to see them for myself and get some pictures. There was no one there when I visited. And I know that there are some things out there in the dark that we just cannot explain. God know who they are and what they are doing, and they will stand in judgment for those things which they have done. Just as the Devil himself they too shall be cast into the lake of fire.

Revelation 20:10
"And the devil that deceived them was cast into the lake of fire and brimstone, where the beast and the false prophet are, and shall be tormented day and night for ever and ever."

Luke 8:17
"For nothing is secret, that shall not be made manifest; neither any thing hid, that shall not be known and come abroad."
Fear not, we know how the book ends. Amen!

Urban Legends of Lincoln County Missouri

3

HOOT OWL HOLLOW

The year is 1920 and prohibition has just started. For the next thirteen years there will not be any alcohol allowed in the United States. On December 5th 1933 that was ended prohibition was over, but many cities had decided to continue to keep alcohol out. Troy, Missouri was one such city, there was to be no alcohol sold, bought or drank within the city limits.

Our story begins just outside of the Troy city limits, where three bars popped up almost overnight. One of those bars was off highway 61 on the rural highway KK, another was on a small road off of highway 47 called Spinster Road and the third was off east highway 47 on a road called Hoot Owl Hollow.

A few weeks ago a woman that goes to my church pulled me to the side one Sunday after service. She told me about some weird things going on out on Hoot Owl Hollow Road and that as an investigative journalist that I might ought to take a look into it. So I did just that.

After knocking on a few doors in the area a man and wife invited me into their home to have a talk about their happenings. The husband proceeded to tell me about strange howling noises that would come and go inside their home. One minute the sound would be downstairs in the basement and when they would go to search it out then it would come from above them in the upstairs. And this had been going on for over twenty years! Of course the family asked that I do no share their names.

Another family in the area said that they often stack their firewood on their porch and every time the next day it will be scattered on the ground.

This was just enough to pique my curiosity and caused me to dig deeper. I searched and managed to find a great-niece of a person that used to own ground out on Hoot Owl Hollow. She is living in a local nursing home, but agreed to talk with me.

This is the story of deceit and murder that she retold to me. In the year 1945 there was a young man by the name of Jesse Smith, he was around 23 years old and was a good looking fellow. He stood about 6'3" and had the darkest hair and the bluest eyes you had ever seen. He probably weighed about 180 pounds and had not a pinch of fat on him.

Now Jesse was born to a well-to-do family from the Union Township just north of Troy, Missouri. So Jesse didn't have to go out and work hard like everyone else did. Jesse took advantage of this by taking advantage of many working men's wives. While they were out earning a living Jesse was sneaking around Troy with their women. As with any lie the husbands found out, but there were about five or so who decided that they were going to take matters into their own hands. Now these men were not your average working men either. They were well known in the community, high profile good-old-boys, and they had had enough.

One night they decided to go out and pay Jesse a visit at his favorite haunt, the bar on Hoot Owl Hollow Road. And that is what they did. They sat in the lot waiting for Jesse to walk out late that night. The moment he stepped out his fate was sealed, they grabbed him and dragged him behind the bar, and began beating him, but it had already gone too far. Jesse fell to the ground and cracked his skull dying instantly. It is said that they dug a hole and buried him right there behind the bar.

The next day his family reached out to the Sheriff and started a search party, but he was never found. Rumor has it that he never will be found as his murderers have too many connections. Jesse Smith and his secrets have been buried until now. It is said that Jesse's spirit will never rest until his killers are brought to justice and his remains returned to his family. So if your ever out on Hoot Owl Hollow watch out because Jesse is still not laid to rest.

Is this just a legend or is it true? You have to make up your own mind.

John 8:7

"And said unto them, He that is without sin among you, let him first cast a stone at her."

Deuteronomy 32:35

"It is mine to avenge; I will repay. In due time their foot will slip; their day of disaster is near and their doom rushes upon them."

Romans 12:17-19

"Do not repay anyone evil for evil. Be careful to do what is right in the eyes of everyone. If it is possible, as far as it depends on you, live at peace with everyone. Do not take revenge, my dear friends, but leave room for God's wrath, for it is written: "It is mine to avenge; I will repay," says the Lord."

The exact site where Hoot Owl Hollow Tavern stood, and unjustified blood was shed.

4

FRENCHMAN'S BLUFF

This reporter went out and dug up, from your local legends, the story of Frenchman's Bluff. Many around this area are familiar with the bluff area on the western edge of Cuivre River State Park outside the city of Troy in Lincoln County Missouri. The bluff area is a common lover's leap type area where young lovers go to sneak a few moments by themselves. Troy is a fair sized town, as of 2017 it had a population of just over 12,000 and it is the county seat.

But let's get into the story of Frenchman's Bluff. In the 1800's a well-to-do frenchman owned all the land around the bluff. He had seen the lack of shops in the local area and had set up a small store and a trading post of sorts. On one fine summer's day he was tending to his store when an Indian chief and his daughter came into the store.

From the very moment the Frenchman laid his eyes upon her face he was spellbound by her. Her beauty was as the majestic eagle soaring in the heavens. He let the Chief have anything he wanted from the store and did not charge him anything. As the Chief readied himself to leave, the Frenchman asked if he could load up his wagon full of supplies, jewelry and valuables and bring them to the camp that night as a gift. It was his hopes to see the beautiful Indian Princess again.

After she had left the image of her was imprinted on his mind. The minutes seemed like hours as the day dragged on until the time when he could close the store, and feast his eyes on her again. Finally the moment was there when he could hurry the last customer out and get on his way. He quickly loaded his wagons with goods and headed for the Indian camp.

As he drove into the camp a line of warriors stood watching him intensely, as if he was a disease that they didn't want to catch. In his mind though it seemed more like they wanted to rid themselves of the disease. But the Frenchman steadily rode on past the line of warriors and straight to the Chief was sitting next to a campfire. He couldn't help but notice the beautiful maiden sitting next to her father.

The Frenchman stepped down from his wagon politely making conversation with the Chief. The language was easy for him as he had learned it many years before. Finally he decided to tell the Chief why he was there.

"My good Chief," He said. "I will happily trade all the goods in my wagon for your daughter's hand in marriage."

But the Chief would not accept, he only insisted that it was against their tribal laws to allow marriage outside of their tribe. The Frenchman refused to accept that answer. He began offering the Chief everything that he had. His home, his land, even his store, it didn't matter to him whatever the Chief asked he would have given it for the woman that sat watching this exchange.

The Chief remained steadfast. No was his answer and it wasn't going to change. He sent the Frenchman away with a warning to never return. As the Frenchman pulled himself up onto the seat of the wagon he vowed unto himself that he would be with the Indian Princess.

Back at home the Frenchman lay in his bed thinking of nothing but her. In the early morning hours he rose from his restlessness. "As the heavens give rain for the grass to live, her love gives me life. Without her I am nothing." And with that he left for the Indian encampment.

As he approached the silent camp he thought on how it had looked earlier that day. He remembered seeing which tepees people had come and gone from, he was certain he knew which one was hers. He sneaked quietly through the camp and to the tepee, peeking inside he could see her sleeping peacefully in the firelight. He stepped inside, bending down he whispered his love for her. She open her eyes and he could see his love and affection reflected there. She took his hand and looked at him questioningly, she knew that her father would never allow this.

"Run away with me." Was all he said. She quickly rose and began wrapping her few belongings in a quilt.

They were almost free from the camp when something dropped from her belongings and clattered to the ground. The warriors who were standing guard let out a fierce war cry, alerting the entire encampment. The young couple ran for the Frenchman's wagon which had been parked a little way from the camp. They jumped onto it and he cracked the whips, his horses sprang to life and bolted forward. It wasn't enough, the Indian warriors on their horses were gaining on them fast. They rode onward hoping to somehow outrun the warriors.

The horse pulling the wagon halted suddenly tossing the couple violently. They jumped from the wagon and saw the open air in front of them as they overlooked the cliff with the fields down below. The two joined hands knowing that this would be the end, there was no escape in either direction.

The tears flowed down the beautiful maiden's cheeks as she looked into the eyes of her love. "We cannot be together in this world, so at least we will be together in the afterlife."

As the rising sun lit the sky they took their final look into each other's eyes. Pressing their lips together in their first kiss they said goodbye.

Now many people say that the Indian warriors threw them to their deaths, but I like to think that just maybe they jumped together in hopes of a new life after this one had ended. Rumor says that if you got to the top of the bluff around 5:30 am that you can see them walking hand in hand along the Cuivre River.

Song of Solomon 8: 6-7

"Set me as a seal upon thine heart, as a seal upon thine arm: for love is strong as death; jealousy is cruel as the grave: the coals thereof are coals of fire, which hath a most vehement flame. Many waters cannot quench love, neither can the floods drown it: if a man would give all the substance of his house for love, it would utterly be contemned."

Urban Legends of Lincoln County Missouri

5

MAJOR CHRISTOPHER CLARK

Pour yourself a cup of hot coffee, settle into your recliner and take a trip back in time with me to when things were much simpler. Back when there was no Highway 61, no Moscow Mills and no Troy, Missouri. Back to when the first white man crossed the big creek with his wagon and his family, into a land filled with wildlife and savages. This brave man was Major Christopher Columbus Clark. The Native Americans that knew this man called him 'Big Hands' because of a fight he had with one of theirs over a rifle,(but that's an entirely different story.) He built his cabin right about where the First Baptist Church now sits in Moscow Mills, and right down from his home was the spring that he was buried next to, this is now where the concrete plant is. Let's journey back and I will tell you about the first man that came to Lincoln County, Missouri, before it even came to be known as Lincoln County!

Christopher Columbus Clark was born August 15th 1768 in Lincoln County, North Carolina. His father James Clark had been a native of Ireland and his mother Kathleen from Scotland, the two having seven boys. Christopher married young and himself had six children with his wife Elizabeth Adam. He served as a lieutenant in a company of volunteers who were guarding the frontiers of Kentucky.

In 1799, at the age of 31 he brought his wife, children and livestock and settled in a place that is now known as Gilmore Spring, Missouri. After having been there only a few days his wife took ill and quickly passed away.

Clark remained at Gilmore Spring for almost a full year before he packed up and moved again. At the age of 33 in 1801 he became the first white man to cross the big creek with his wagons and settled at the very edge of what is now known as Lincoln County, Missouri. From what is known of his homestead, he settled and built his home right where the First Baptist Church in Moscow Mills now sits, about three and a half miles south of Troy. In 1804 at the age of 36 he married his second wife, a young woman from Virginia named Hetty, with whom he had another three children.

That same year of 1804 Governor William Henry Harrison commissioned Christopher Clark as Captain of the volunteers and he was sworn in to service February of 1805 at the age of 37. At that time there was a small settlement of Sac and Fox Indians in the area that they had been ordered to protect the people from. Then came 1812 as the war arose the settlers wasted no time building small forts to protect their homes. Captain Clark built a stockade at his residence and it was commonly called Clark Fort. Then in the Indian war of 1812 many of the Ranger volunteers from the area served under Captain Christopher Clark. Finally in 1815 the war came to an end and life went back to normal.

In December of 1818 Captain Clark and the state officials all met at the state capital in St. Charles to decide on what this county would be named. Captain Clark was not a very good public speaker, but he knew that he would have to speak now. So he arose and these are his words, "Dear Mr. Speaker, I was the first to bring a wagon across the big creek, and I was the first white man to live on the boundary of this new county. Now I was born in Lincoln County, North Carolina, then I moved to Lincoln County, Kentucky and if God is willing, I would like to die in Lincoln County, Missouri." Then he again took his seat. And that is exactly what the decided to name the new county, Lincoln County, Missouri.

In August of 1819 Christopher Columbus Clark and his friend David Lord Al Moore Cotner were granted a license to keep a bar and to run a distillery, the fee to open the establishment was ten dollars per man. The two ran the bar and distillery together until the death of Christopher Columbus Clark on September 17th of 1841, when he was 73 years old. His death was a great loss to the community and his name will never be forgotten.

6

THE CHRISTMAS ORPHAN TRAIN

A whole lot of people have the wrong idea when it comes to the meaning of Christmas. Now when I think of Christmas I think about love, kindness, giving and sharing. But so many people in this day only think that it is about receiving when it is truly about giving from the kindness of your heart.

Over 2000 years ago a baby boy was born in a tiny manger in Bethlehem. From the very moment that he came to this earth he gave. This blessed baby was named Jesus. He gave sight to the blind, hearing to the deaf, he healed the lame and even raised the dead. The biggest sacrifice that he gave was his very own life, when he died on the cross so that we could be forgiven. He then laid in the tomb for three days and rose on the third day to give us eternal life. His birth, life and death were all about giving.

"Greater love hath no man than this, that a man lay down his life for his friends" -John 15:13

This Christmas story is about two very different families here in Troy, Missouri who opened up their homes to unwanted children. In the year 1854 the streets of New York City were brimming with homeless and orphaned children. With only the clothes on their backs they wandered the streets and spent their nights foraging through trash cans hoping to find a small morsel of food, some were even lucky enough to catch a rat or two for their meal.

It came to a crisis point because there were so many of these children, that city officials didn't know what to do. But a social worker named Charles Loring Brace had an idea. He decided to put these children on trains headed west so that families outside of the city might have a chance to adopt them. So, that is exactly what they did! Between the years 1854 and 1929 more than 250,000 orphans were shipped from New York City out west.

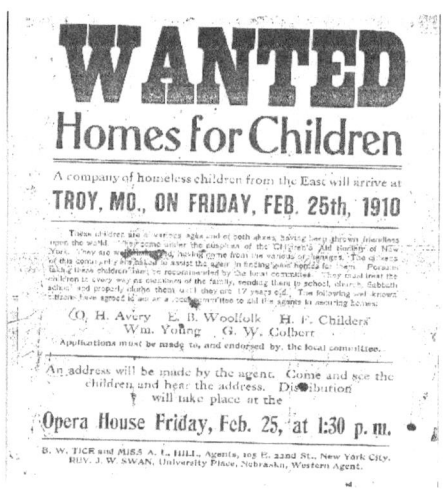

Now you might ask yourself, 'What does that have to do with Troy, Missouri?' Well I'll tell you. On February 25th 1910 one of those trains stopped right here in little old

Troy. There were two families who stepped up and each took a child. Unfortunately in life not everything would turn out as we would like for it to. While one of these stories is a blessing the other is not. One family wanted to give the gift of love while the other wanted to simply receive the gift of free labor.

"And above all these things put on charity, which is the bond of perfectness."- Colossians 3: 14

Philip Kuhne a machinist and his wife Lenora took in four-year-old John M. K. Monahan. They already had a child five-year-old Camille, but they made room in their home and in their hearts for one more. John took their last name and they changed his first name from John to Philip. The family took in this young boy and raised him as their own in a home full of love and tenderness. This was the story of giving and receiving love from a child that had never known love before.

When you give, don't expect anything in return, but God will bless you for giving.

Will A. Howell a farmer and his wife Daisy decided to open up their home to a seven-year-old named Theodore Smith, but sadly he was not lucky like John was. The exact reasons are unknown, but after some time it was discovered that Theodore was not living with his adopted parents. He was found some years later living in the next town, Theodore and another runaway boy were found living in an abandoned house half-starved. Details are scant and after this account he seems to just disappear into time.

This Christmas when you gather around your tree rather than thinking on what you can get from other people, try thinking on the joy that you can give instead. Open your hearts and maybe even your homes to those children out there who have no family to love them.2 Corinthians 9:6

"But this I say, He which soweth sparingly shall reap also sparingly; and he which soweth bountifully shall reap also bountifully."

Acts 20:35

"I have shewed you all things, how that so labouring ye ought to support the weak, and to remember the words of the Lord Jesus, how he said, It is more blessed to give than to receive."

Deuteronomy 10: 18

"He doth execute the judgment of the fatherless and widow, and loveth the stranger, in giving him food and raiment."

7

THE ORPHAN TRAIN FOLLOW UP

As many of you will remember that during this past Christmas holiday I wrote a story about the Orphan Train. It was a tale of people opening their heart to a child that had no home. And for those of you who don't know about the Orphan Train I will share a few of the details.

Back in the mid to late 1800's and into the early 1900's orphans from New York were put on trains headed for the mid-west. In the approximately seventy-five years that this went on somewhere near half a million children were shipped to the middle of the country in the hopes of finding a home. It is believed that somewhere around 100,000 of those came into Missouri. Many of these children were from broken homes, or low income families but a good majority of them had simply abandoned to the city streets. These were children with no one to depend on other than themselves, they would sell newspapers and beg for food, whatever they could do just to survive another day.

The story I shared was about one of these children named John M. K. Monahan. He had been born sometime around 1906 to his mother and father John T. and Sophia Monahan. Not long after the baby john had been born his mother passed away. His father seeing no other way to turn took him to a hospital that would take in orphans and left him.At the age of four John was put on a train packed with other children and shipped West to Missouri. It was a cold, snowy February 25th in 1910 when John stepped off the train to meet his new parents in Troy, Missouri. Imagine that scared little four year old boy, terrified and confused not knowing what to expect. Philip Kuhne and his wife Lenora ran a small mercantile store with his family on Main Street right in the middle of Troy. These two stood waiting with open arms and open hearts to greet their new little boy.

Sadly other orphans were not so lucky. Some of the families would take in the children only to treat them like slaves, and work them from sun up to sun down. Many of the orphans that came into these families would simply run away. Their stories lost and records of them unable to be found.

But sweet little John Monahan was one of the lucky ones. Philip and Lenora had a child of their own who was also under five at the time, her name was Camille. The family legally had John's last name changed to theirs. Now John M. K. Kuhne, he grew up happy working with the family in the store. He stayed there until Philip closed the store sometime around the late 1950's or early 1960's. Philip Kuhne was born in 1869 and passed away at the age of 73, and was buried in the Troy Cemetery.

Once the store was closed John took a job working for the Post Office delivering mail until he retired at the age of sixty-five. In 1979 when John M. K. Kuhne was 74 years old he passed away and was buried in the Troy Cemetery just like his dad before him. John lived a good life and everyone who knew him loved him. He was also a very religious man, and was a member in good standing with the Methodist Church in Troy. John and his wife had three children, they even named their middle child Philip after John's adopted dad.

This story just goes to show you that one wrong turn can make your life a disaster, but on the other had one right turn can take that disaster and make it into a blessing. Most of this story was only recently told to me by John's second child, Philip. Philip is now eighty years old, retired from McDonnell Douglas and lives in St. Louis County with his wife. This reporter would like to thank you, Philip, for all of your help.

God is the great protector and loving Father to all children living as orphans.

Psalm 68:5
"A father of the fatherless, and a judge of the widows, is God in his holy habitation."
He who numbers even the hairs of our head will certainly not turn away from the children living as orphans, and this should inspire up to act in the same manner.

John Monahan Kuhne

8

THE BOHEMIAN SETTLEMENT

As we all come together for Thanksgiving this story should warm your heart. It's about a little ghost town that used to sit on a hill about halfway between Hawk Point and Troy. The little town was called Mashek and it was nestled quietly out on what is now Hwy AA. Nothing of the town remains except for the graveyard overlooking the valley where the people used to live. This is the story of one Bohemian family who carried their hopes and dreams all the way from the other side of the world to settle here in Lincoln County, Mo.

The story was recounted to me by two of the Bohemian ladies who still live in the area. This is the way they had heard it all their life.

'This is the story of our family and their journey. The journey towards a better life and new opportunities. Farming was our life. It was our hopes and dreams, our livelihood, everything we had was tied up in farming. Our family lived in Pilsni by Prague in Bohemia. Then one year there came a drought, but it did not stop, the drought continued on for many years afterward. There was no rain, and no rain meant no crops. And with no crops the food started to become scarce. It had become apparent to us that we would have to move to the city. We moved to Prague where we all were able to get jobs. And while we had plenty to live on and we had food and clothes, we were not happy. We were farmers and the city life was not for us.

Then came some news about a ship that was bound for America. We headed to the little church outside of town to pray about this news. It would be a life altering decision if we decided to go. Then, yes we decided to pack up and leave for America. We boarded the ship with mixed emotions with doubt and concerns about the future, and even some joy. But we were now leaving behind our relatives and friends, our country. But we were going to America! We took with us only the bare necessities, our clothes, pictures and treasured memories, and every man had his fiddle. Yes, we Bohemians love music and dancing, and of course our fiddles. It was a long trip and the conditions on board were horrible, unsanitary and disease infested.'

Isaiah 43:2

"When thou passest through the waters, I will be with thee; and through the rivers, they shall not overflow thee: when thou walkest through the fire, thou shalt not be burned; neither shall the flame kindle upon thee."

After many weeks we finally saw land, America! When we got our feet on solid ground we took a look around in horror. It was nothing like we thought it was going to be. It was a big muddy mess and the people went around jabbering in a language that we did not understand. The were speaking English not Bohemian. But, we were in America. First thing we set out to find jobs so that we would be able to afford the necessities. After several months in New Orleans we set sail up the Mississippi River for St. Louis, Missouri.

Once there we met with a man named Mr. Block. He was a real estate man, and he said that he would be able to find what we needed, which was tillable land, woods and a spring. We waited while Mr. Block searched. It wasn't long before he returned to us and said that he had found the perfect place. So, once again we set sail up the Mississippi River then onto the Cuivre River. After landing we got off the boat and climbed a small hill, we looked around and saw that the land was beautiful. There we were, our family with only the bare necessities looking at just what we had wanted, beautiful farmland, plenty of woods and even a little spring.

It was 1862 when we started out, and the first thing we did was to build a little log church. Then we planted gardens and started clearing the land for crops, in the meantime we hunted the woods for the abundant squirrels and rabbits. The waters were full of fish and the woods full of grapes. We were happy to be farmers again!

Eventually the little village grew, we even had a small store that sold the essentials like coffee, tobacco and sugar. Every once in a while a peddler would come through with their merchandise. It was 1886 when the old log church had to be tore down and a nice church was built. The old logs were used to build the new town hall where we had our meetings and dances, even the farmers used it to discuss their crops. Next to the town hall the store was built with a small post office in it. With the addition of the post office the town of Mashek, Missouri was established. Then came a blacksmith and even the Cottonwood Distillery.

But like most things in life came change. The people began to move away to Troy, Hawk Point and even the bigger cities to try to find work and slowly the town faded into the past.

In 1963 the church was tore down. And now a new generation is moving into the area, subdivisions are springing up around the hill and the beautiful countryside disappearing. The cemetery stills sits proudly on the hilltop quietly keeping watch over the Bohemian settlement.

We are proud to be American! It was a long trip to get here, but it was worth every hardship.'

Isaiah 40:31

"But they that wait upon the Lord shall renew their strength; they shall mount up with wings as eagles; they shall run, and not be weary; and they shall walk, and not faint."

Urban Legends of Lincoln County Missouri

9

OLD MONROE HOBGOBLIN

In the eastern section of Lincoln County, Missouri lies the sleepy little town of Old Monroe. Not a lot goes on in Old Monroe it's just your average quiet town with nothing to do. But all of that just might be about to change! Some of the local folk whom I have been talking to have told me eerie tales. Tales about the ghost of a devil walking the streets of Old Monroe late at night. It's hard to say whether they truly saw it or not, maybe they had drank a little too much, or possibly the shadows were shifting just right in the wind. We may never truly know.

And so the story goes, it was a cold February night in 1894. The snow was falling lightly and just starting to blanket the streets. Now William Bothe and his brother Henry were both known to be responsible and well respected citizens of the community, they were both known to be in sound mind and known for their honesty. The people in the community believed the brothers even though they were talking about something unbelievable.

And the story that they told was unbelievable. They said that they were walking down the road and as they passed the Lutheran Church a rat ran past them, just as fast as it could. Henry was laughing so loud about the rat when it came right next to them and ran under the fence on the side of the road. But it was at that exact moment when the Old Monroe Hobgoblin made his appearance. Henry immediately began to shake like a leaf as his face turned as white as the freshly fallen snow. He could barely stutter out the words that he had just seen a devil. When he recounted the tale later he said that he knew it was a devil because it's eyes were flashing and they were as bright as the noonday sun. The creature, he said, had to have stood a good eight feet tall, and it's body was not like a human's at all, it was the body of some misshapen twisted creature. Then it made the wretched laugh, like some sort of demented thing crying out for his blood. Henry turned and ran, forgetting all about his poor brother William and leaving him behind. He said that he ran so fast that not even his own breath could catch him.

Now if it had just been the Bothe brothers who had witnessed this demon it might have just been laughed off and forgotten. But a short while later another fellow in the community saw the Hobgoblin too. It was late at night, some say that it was just about midnight when a good man by the name of Mr. Burkemper was walking right past the Lutheran Church. His feet almost froze to the ground when he heard a terrible wailing of some sort of spirit not far off. He listened for a moment wondering to himself as to what it could have been. It was then that he looked up the street and saw the most horrible sight that he had ever seen in his entire life. It was the hobgoblin running down the road straight for him. Mr. Burkemper said that he turned and ran away so fast that he nearly ran right out of his shoes.

Well a few farmers in the area had heard about this goblin, and they decided that they had heard enough and were going to take matters into their own hands. They got together one night at one of their old farm houses and stayed up late tossing ideas around as to what they were going to do about this demon. They came up with everything that they could think of from hunting dogs to bear traps. This was when one of the older farmers thought it might be better for them to just load up their shotguns, pile into theirs wagons and go down the Lutheran Church and wait for it to show it's ugly face and then blow it off.

So that is what they decided to do. They waited until it was good and late as the hours ticked closer to midnight they all piled into one of their wagons and headed over to where the sightings had happened. The old wood wagon rattled down the road with enough weapons and angry farmers in it to scare off anyone. But the looks of the wagon were deceiving, the men inside it were just as scared as the witnesses had been. You probably could have heard their teeth chattering a half mile away. Even though it was only around 15 degrees outside all the men in the wagon were sweating.

They sat and waited for what seemed like an eternity before the goblin finally showed up. At first it was just the horrible wailing, then the saw it's glowing eyes, then it's grotesque body and the horns that stuck up from it's head. It pranced and snorted as the farmers quaked with fear and muttered silent prayers. One farmer turned and ran as fast as his legs would carry him, a second one could do nothing other than squeak. The third raised his double barrel shotgun and unloaded it at the beast.

A human voice screamed from the creature, "Don't shoot! Stop, Stop!" and then it told them it's name as it pulled off it's mask.

And that is why the Old Monroe Hobgoblin snorts and wails no more. It was all a practical joke! A young man in the neighborhood had set it all up to make himself look like a beast and practiced making monkey noises to sound unearthly. He was truly lucky as the shotgun blast had missed him by only inches. I have included a picture that the Post Dispatch had drawn back when they did a write up on the Hobgoblin many years ago, but everyone says that it doesn't look much like the real thing.

2 Corinthians 4:2
"We have renounced secret and shameful ways; we do not use deception, nor do we distort the word of God. On the contrary, by setting forth the truth plainly we commend ourselves to everyone's conscience in the sight of God."

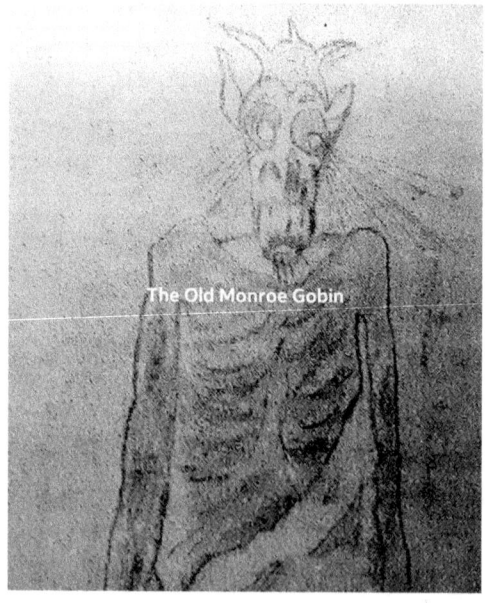

The Old Monroe Gobin

10

OAK RIDGE CEMETERY

Just two miles from Elsberry, Missouri, on a big hill overlooking beautiful rolling valleys sits Oak Ridge Cemetery. Horrifying tales have come out of this little graveyard. According to onlyinyourstate.com it is the 8th most haunted cemetery in the state of Missouri. These claims were enough to cause this reporter to drive on over to Elsberry and see if the title of 8th most haunted cemetery was well earned.

It was in front of the Dollar General that I met up with a woman who had the whitest hair I had ever seen. She stared at me, a wad of chewing tobacco in her bottom lip, and told me that her name was Ruby. She gave a big spit and began her tale.

Sadly, our story begins at the end of someone else's. It was Halloween in the year of 1930 and a very wealthy old woman named Alice just passed away. Now Alice was only 98 years old, but folks said that she looked more like she was a hundred and fifty years old.

And so the legend goes that Alice's last request was for all of her precious jewelry to be put to rest in the grave with her when she died. That Halloween day almost a million dollars worth of jewelry was buried with that little old woman. She had said that the reason for this request was that she did not want any one else to have to go through what she had gone through. Alice told her friends that there was a curse on her jewelry and she didn't want anyone else to have to endure the pain that she had suffered.When Alice was a much younger woman she had gone to a bank auction and bought all the jewelry they had for sale. Unknowingly she had bought the adornments of a witch named Gwendolyn. This witch had put a mighty curse on the jewels stating that whoever bought them would suffer terribly. Not only would they live a long life watching everyone that they loved pass on before them, but they would have to feel the physical pain of their loved one's deaths.

Now back to the cemetery. The Oak Ridge Cemetery in that day had an odd caretaker. A woman named Mary Lou lived in a small shack on the grounds and took care of things within the cemetery grounds. Mary Lou was about fifty years old and was rather reclusive.

She didn't like to talk to other people, but would often go around talking to and even answering herself.

People called her a 'mumbler'. Regardless of her oddness Mary Lou was a good hard worker who caringly tended to the cemetery.

When Mary Lou was told about Alice being buried with all of her jewelry she said to herself, 'Not on my watch!' As she determined to patrol the cemetery every hour on the hour to ward off grave robbers. She prepared her lantern and put on some coffee, she knew it was going to be a long night.

Patrol after patrol she went making her way around the cemetery and then back to her little shack. She had just made her midnight round when she came back to her front door. As she opened the door two men grabbed her and pulled her inside.

The next day they found Mary Lou's body standing on the top of her shack overlooking the cemetery. The inside of her home was a scene right from a horror movie. A bloody hammer lay in the middle of the floor and splashes of red around the room.

No one was sure why they tied her body standing upright on the roof, but I think it was to spite her by making her watch them steal the jewelry.

They say that since that day, if you wait until the midnight hour that Mary Lou still walks the cemetery with her lantern in hand. And if you listen closely you just might her her mumble as she walks slowly making her rounds. It is said that she will not rest until all of Alice's jewelry is found and brought back to the grave where it had been laid to rest. And my warning to you is to beware when you buy expensive jewelry as it may be cursed.

Galatians 3:13

"Christ hath redeemed us from the curse of the law, being made a curse for us: for it is written, Cursed is every one that hangeth on a tree."

11

SATAN'S TUNNEL

In rural Lincoln County, Missouri sits the little town of Hawk Point. The town is so named for the many hawks that used to nest in the area of the original town site. The 669 people of Hawk Point are served by a Post Office which has been around since 1840.

That's the history that most everybody knows. And if you enjoy boring stuff like that, you might as well quit reading now, because this reporter is seeking for the things that you don't know the history of.

In this quiet little town of Hawk Point are many hidden secrets that the townsfolk like to keep 'Hush Hush'. But this reporter went and dragged out one of the biggest hidden secrets and is going to uncover and reveal it's mysteries to you.

In the nearby countryside it lies waiting for some curiously innocent teenager, or a homeless person looking for some shelter from the cold. Many people have gone here, but not as many have returned from the clutches of 'Satan's Tunnel'.

Now Satan's Tunnel is a dark gloomy place, just stepping into it's shadow causes the chills to creep up your spine. A thick scent akin to death hangs in the air as a bitter nasty taste fills the back of your throat, and won't go away. I have been there, and I have no desire what-so-ever to go back. The feeling of death lingers there.

This long tunnel used to have railroad tracks that went over top of it, but the stories began before the railroads ran through the area. Legend goes that there used to be a group of gypsies in the area. It is told that they had claimed the area where the tunnel now sits as theirs. Late at night they would go to their 'sacred' hill and light their bonfires. As the nights would draw on kidnapped children would be sacrificed as the gypsies sang and danced. It is even told that somewhere in the surrounding woods is a hidden cemetery where the gypsies buried the poor little children that fell victim to their cruel rituals.

Much later after the gypsies were scattered and the tracks laid in their place, people claimed that they would often hear the sounds of revelry mingled with the cries of terrified children as they traveled through the area.

One such tale speaks of a man, almost a century ago. He ventured along the tracks late one evening to investigate the claims of terrible sounds in the night. When he didn't return, people went looking for him. His body laid at the mouth of the tunnel, thrown there from the tracks some twenty feet above him. Had something drawn his attention so that he didn't hear the train coming? No one can say for sure, but it was another victim claimed by the tunnel.

Now a tale of the tunnel from the 70's to chill you to the bone. It was in the late years of this decade when a group of teenagers from nearby Hawk Point decided to have a party out at the tunnel. One of the kids reported that things were just getting started when he looked up and saw a dark figure approaching them. As it came closer he could see that it was haggard old man, he was speaking in a low grumbling voice. "Leave this place and never come back. Evil waits here."

He just kept repeating it over and over again. "Leave this place and never come back. Evil waits here." He appeared to have completely lost his mind. He spoke of frightening stories of death and terror, of people claimed by the tunnel and thrown from the tracks. He told them of demons in the woods and horrors waiting for them if they didn't leave this place now.

The teens decided to leave, they tried to get the old man to come with them. "I can never leave, I am bound to this ground. The spirits hold me here." He repeated over again and again has he wandered from the party. With their spirits dampened the kids scattered and went home.

After a few days a couple of them were able to get some adults to listen to their tale and follow them out to the tunnel to look for the old man. He was found in the black center of the tunnel, his face twisted in an expression of terror on his face. One more for the tunnel.

A final tale and I will put this article to rest, unlike the spirits at Satan's Tunnel. A local man told his family that he was going to go for an early afternoon walk in the woods near his home. He didn't return. His family sent out a search party in the morning. They looked all around for him, but he was nowhere to be found. They had almost given up hope when finally he was spotted on the hill above the tunnel. His body swinging from a rope strung up in an old oak tree. Apparently he had hung himself in the night. They say that if you go to the tunnel on the right day of the year, at sunset as the light begins to fail, that you can see his shadow swinging back and forth from that old tree.But in a world of such thing we must remember what the Lord says.

Deuteronomy 31:6

"Be strong and courageous. Do not be afraid or terrified because of them, for the LORD your God goes with you; he will never leave you nor forsake you."

Remember to never fear and to stand strong as 'Christians', the devil cannot take any thing from you unless you give it to him first.

12

RESTLESS SPIRITS

The love between a parent and child is the purest, deepest form of love that one could ever imagine. A love so strong that it could cause the dead to be restless and wander in search of their children forever. Or so that is how this story goes. It is said that there are two restless spirits that wander the hilltops that overlook the Sugar Creek in Cuivre River State Park. Hand in hand the will forever search for their ten children that were never laid to rest in the family grave site. That is where David Duey and his wife Mary both are buried on a hilltop in the middle of what is now the state park.

David was born in 1812 in Jackson County, West Virginia. Shortly after David was born his parents split up, they then decided to give him to a couple that was childless. At the tender age of six years old his foster parents decided to move from West Virginia to St. Louis, Missouri.

David lived in St. Louis until his foster father died, he then moved to Troy, Missouri with his foster mother until she later passed away. It was soon after that he met his wife, Mary. It was love at first sight. They were quickly married and went on to have ten children, nine boys and one girl. David also helped to establish the first Christian Church in Troy. David was a good man who faithfully served God and his family. One of his children, Beverly Duey even grew up to become the Lincoln County Sheriff. David passed away on December 27th 1858. There are no details as to how he died. He was then buried just about a quarter of a mile from his homestead on a hilltop nearby to Sugar Creek in Lincoln County, Missouri. Mary passed away 22 years after her husband in the year 1880. Beside their stones are set ten smaller ones for their children that never came home to be buried.

It had been the greatest wish of David that even in death that the family would remain together. But for some reason or another not a single one of their children was buried there. They say that as long as their children are not brought to the parents graveyard that David and Mary with remain eternally restless, wandering forevermore in search of their missing children.

If you too are restless and wish to seek out the grave site of the Duey family I suggest you bring your hiking boots, plenty of water and your lunch and certainly don't forget the bug repellent. It took this reporter from 11a.m. to almost 6:30p.m. to find them.

Proverbs 6:20

"My son, keep thy father's commandment, and forsake not the law of thy mother."

1 Timothy 5:8

"But if any provide not for his own and specially for those of his own house, he has denied the faith, and is worse than an unbeliever."

Urban Legends of Lincoln County Missouri

13

RESTLESS SPIRITS FOLLOW UP

The story that you are about to hear has been 161 years in the making. The year was 1858 when David Duey was laid to rest and 22 years later his lovely wife Mary was laid beside him. Ten little tombstones set waiting for their children to be buried with their parents, but for one reason or another the children's bodies were never brought home to the parent's graveside. That was until now, three generations later!

I'm sure you all remember the story of the unresting spirits of Sugar Creek. That story did so much more than just touch the hearts of the people of Lincoln County, Missouri. It reached all the way over into Edwardsville, Illinois straight to Jim, the great-great-great-grandson to David Duey!

Here about two weeks ago I received a call from a man saying that he had read the story of the Sugar Creek spirits and that he was one of the grandchildren. He asked me if I could draw him a map and said that he would try to find his way to it, somehow. I told him, 'No, way. I started this story and I am going to see it through to it's end. I will take you out there personally.'

Now Jim was really excited about that. He told me that he had heard about his ancestor's graves all of his life, but no one actually knew where they were at. It had been shrouded in mystery for all these years! I told Jim to come on over whenever he was ready and I would show the graves to him. October 22nd at the ranger station in Cuivre River State park, with a chilly wind blowing, I met Jim in person around ten in the morning. We greeted each other and made small talk for a few minutes, but I knew what was on Jim's mind. He wanted to see the graves.

Back into the State Park and deep into the woods we went, once again looking for the final resting place of David and Mary Duey. My first trip out there almost killed me, but to unite this man with his grandfather was certainly something that I would do this hike again for. It was a long hike and we were both wore out by the time we finally got there.

As we approached the graves I watched as Jim's eyes brightened with a light of happiness. It was almost as if he was reborn with a burst of energy. I knew that he felt a warmness come over his body in the moment as we stood there in silence just looking at the graves, I could feel the warmth too. Jim had finally found what he had been searching for, for many years.

I could tell that it was a very emotional moment for him as Jim pulled a bouquet of flowers from his backpack and placed them on his Grandfather's grave, and then he pulled out a second bouquet and placed those on his Grandmother's grave. At that moment I could feel the tears begin to well up in my eyes, I held them back event though I knew that the man at the gravesides felt the same way too. We stood in a revered silence for at least ten minutes before Jim turned to me and said that he was ready to go.

Back at our cars we talked briefly and Jim said that he was going to bring his daughters and his brother out so that they could see them too. He told me how he might even like to look into have the stone re-surfaced. Soon we said our good-byes and got into our cars. It was after one-thirty in the afternoon as I began to pull away. The time of silence spent at the graveside lingered in my mind, and I knew that It would be in Jim's too.

I believe that there is a reason to everything that happens in life. There was a reason that I wrote that story, and there is a reason that Jim had to come to Missouri and visit his long lost grandparent's graves. So reasons we can know and others we may never have the answer for. As I think on life's many reasons, I do think that the unrest spirits of Sugar Creek are finally at rest after 161 years.

Ecclesiastes 3:1-8
"To every thing there is a season, and a time to every purpose under the heaven A time to be born, and a time to die; a time to plant, and a time to pluck up that which is planted; A time to kill, and a time to heal; a time to break down, and a time to build up; A time to weep, and a time to laugh; a time to mourn, and a time to dance; A time to cast away stones, and a time to gather stones together; a time to embrace, and a time to refrain from embracing; A time to get, and a time to lose; a time to keep, and a time to cast away; A time to rend, and a time to sew; a time to keep silence, and a time to speak; A time to love, and a time to hate; a time of war, and a time of peace.

66

14

THE SINKHOLE BATTLE

A battle that should not have been fought, but had to be. It was a meaningless war full of meaningful deaths. The blood that fell on the ground that day should not have been shed, unfortunately for those who lost their lives, it had to be. Well, let us get to the story and then you will understand.

It is May 24th 1815 on the border of what will later become Lincoln and St. Charles Counties. It is a day like any other the sun is up, the birds are singing and flowers are in bloom. A platoon of soldiers have only just set out from a small fort. They are heading to an abandoned cabin to retrieve a grinding stone.

They had only just set out when the platoon came to a halt. Their leader had thought that he heard something in the bushes near the road. After a few moments they set off again, their leader telling himself that it must have been only a squirrel. Beginning again, they had truly only just begun, when the first shots rang out in what would later be known as the Battle of the Sinkhole.

The first fallen soldier was Francois Lammey, then Antoine Pelker, and Hubbard Tayon. The Indians were picking them off like flies upon the wall. The platoon retreated to the fort, where the Rangers had opened fire upon the Indians, to no avail as they were out of rifle range. Captain Peter Craig rallied the men together and he and forty soldiers headed out to engage the enemy. Captain Peter Craig had come north from Cape Girardeau, he was the son-in-law of famous pioneer Andrew Ramsey Sr. As he and his men approached the Indians began to fall back to the sinkhole to the Northwest of the fort. It wasn't long before the soldiers were joined by another twenty men and Captain David Musick from nearby Fort Independence. Captain Peter Craig was the first man to fall when the fighting resumed, followed by Alexander Giboney Jr. After which the command passed to Lieutenant Edward Spear.

The Sauk Indians were led by a man named Blackhawk, he then led his men to take refuge in the sinkhole. Lieutenant Spears, taking advantage of a moment free of shooting, ordered his men to rig a battery from the pieces of a cart. The resulting structure was able to conceal six men. A crazy command from Lieutenant Spears put the

battery near the edge of the sinkhole, though he didn't realize that this left the men inside unconcealed from below.

The Sauk Indians saw their advantage and easily took aim for the soldiers. Lieutenant Spears suffered a fatal wound, and most of the others inside were wounded as well. As night began to fall and with so many being wounded or lost the remaining soldiers post a guard over the sinkhole and retreated once again to the fort.

At some point in the night Blackhawk and his men escaped, completely eluding the guard. The soldiers surveyed the carnage, eight of their men were dead and five wounded, one man was completely missing. And only one of Blackhawk's men had been killed.

The sad part of this tale is that the war had ended over three months before the Sinkhole Battle, but word had not yet reached the soldiers or Indians in Missouri. Many people could say that these men lost their lives in vain, but I don't think so. If these men had not stood against Blackhawk and his men, they could have easily come further up the Cuivre River into Lincoln County and killed many innocent homesteaders. I thank God for the brave soldiers who stood against Blackhawk and I salute them for their sacrifice.

John 15:13
"Greater love hath no man than this, that a man lay down his life for his friends."

Urban Legends of Lincoln County Missouri

15

SUGAR CREEK WEREWOLF

It's been about a year now since I had gotten that call. I remember it well, the woman was named Lily, but she didn't want to mention her last name so that her neighbors wouldn't think she was crazy. When I talked with her she seemed really reasonable and sounded like she had plenty of common sense. But then she told me one of the weirdest stories that I think I have ever heard.

Lily told me that she is married with two children, a girl and a boy and that they live out on Highway Y North of Troy, Missouri. Well one of Lily's favorite things is to take a long walk every evening along the cliffs that run above Sugar Creek. She would usually wait for her husband to get home so that he could watch the children while she walked and took in the peacefulness and beauty of nature.

On one particular evening a couple of years back her husband was running late getting home, but she happily waited and went for her walk when he arrived, though it was much later than usual. She hopped in the car and headed down to Park Drive and follow it to the lot at the Sugar Creek Trails. She parked the car and headed to a trail that she knew well. The trail starts off going down a big hill then veers left and up another hill. At the top of that hill you go right on a different trail that takes you to the cliffs overlooking Sugar Creek.

At the top of the cliffs Lily sat down to enjoy the sunset view,. Though the sun had already set there was still plenty of light and the moon was already high and full. After a few moments Lily began to realize that she was hearing something coming through the woods on the other side of the creek. It was like something that she had never seen before! She quickly hid behind a tree so she could watch what the creature was doing. As she watched, she realized that it appeared to be half wolf/ half man.

She told me how she remembered standing there hiding behind that tree thinking how crazy this was. Lily watched as it crept out of the woods on all fours, but then stood on it's back two legs as it went into the water. It seemed to be about seven feet all! The creature jumped around splashing in the creek like it was trying to grab at fish. Suddenly it froze and pointed it's nose skyward and began sniffing. Then looked right at her, the beast's eyes glowed red like something straight from the pits of Hell.

The beast howled, a horrific sound like something she had never heard before and ran for the cliff right below where she had been hiding. Lily remembered that she had her .22 pistol in her pack, she pulled it out and fired two rounds right at the creature. It immediately fell from where it was climbing, about ten feet up from the creek. It behaved like it had been hit and she was certain that she could see blood in the water. It hurried for the far back and pulled itself out of the water, raised up on it's back legs then howled again, the sound chilled Lily to her bones. She watched, frozen, as it dropped back down on all four legs and scrambled back into the woods that it had come from.

Lily turned and ran all the way back to her car and rushed home. To this day she has not returned to walk the Sugar Creek trails.

The story seemed crazy to me, so I let it sit not going any further with it until I had some more information or confirmation of the tale. But then a few weeks ago the call came. It was from a man named Billy Dorman, he said to go ahead and use his name because most folks think that he's crazy anyways.

Now Mr. Dorman is retired and spends a good amount of his spare time out gathering rock fossils. He likes to walk the creek beds because that's where he finds most of his best rocks. Late one afternoon he decided to go out to Sugar Creek off of Highway KK and walk it for fossils. It was a cool afternoon and had rained the day before, and after a good rain you find the best rocks from the water turning over the creek bed.

Billy parked his car and started walking Southeast along the creek. He had gathered a few nice fossils when he realized that it was starting to get dark. The dark didn't bother him much because he had his flashlight and knew the area well enough to find his way. He continued along the creek shining his flashlight on the rocks when he came to a deep part of the creek with high cliffs on the one side. A strange noise coming from further up the river made him to stop and listen. It was like a wolf howling at the moon, he looked up and noticed that the moon was big and full. The sound started coming towards him, and fast. Billy said that he ran to the side of the creek and lay down flat in some weeds.

Mr. Dorman could just barely see the creature as it came to the deep pool in the creek, but it seemed to be a wolf/man of about seven or so feet tall and went along on it's hind legs. It stopped in the deeper water and looked around, it's nose in the air sniffing. Billy thought it was going to sniff him out of his hiding place when it lost interest and began splashing around like it was trying to grab at fish, or maybe just washing itself. He didn't know what it was doing and didn't really care, he just wanted it to leave so the he could get out of there and get home where he would be safe! It splashed around for about fifteen minutes before moving back up the creek the way it had come. Billy waited until he couldn't hear it anymore before jumping up and getting back to his car as fast as he could.

Billy Dorman told me that he had told no one about this before calling me. Well this now made two reports of a werewolf in almost exactly the same place, I had to investigate. I headed out Highway KK and parked my car by the bridge unpacked my camping gear and set out for the cliffs along Sugar Creek. It is early September and the weatherman had said that there is supposed to be a full moon this night, but there is a hurricane in the gulf causing some cloudiness here in Missouri. It was around five p.m. when I started out and every step of that almost mile long walk I felt like I was being watched.

It was quiet when I finally made it to where I wanted to camp, the quiet trickle of the creek and soft whispering of the light breeze moving through the trees. I asked my self if I actually expected to find a werewolf and the answer was no, maybe a stray wolf, pack of coyotes or even a territorial bear but certainly not a werewolf. Those are just myths, right?

As I gathered my firewood that eerie feeling of being watched came over me again. I couldn't shake it, I just knew that something was out there, watching me. It wasn't long before the darkness of night overtook the comfort of the daylight, even the full moon hid behind the clouds only peeking out occasionally. I had my fire burning brightly, trying to shake the feeling that something was waiting for me to turn my back to it so that it could pounce on me out of the blackness of the woods.

The forest came alive the later it got, splashes in the creek, twigs breaking, steps and scurries on the forest floor. At every one I jumped and turned hoping to catch a glimpse of the werewolf. Around nine o'clock, something let out a howl and it was close! I scrambled to get my flashlight from my bag to investigate and headed for the woods where the sound had come from. By the time I got myself together and headed over there a second howl came. This time it was on top of the cliff! I knew that there was no way one creature could have moved that fast, so there had to be at least two of them. I hurried back into my camp and built my fire up bigger and got myself ready for bed knowing that there was not going to be any sleep for me this night.

From the safety of my tent I watched out the unzipped door, but hardly got more than a glimpse of nothing more than fast movement. It continued all night. Fast steps around my campsite howling from here and there, occasional growls. Shortly before sunrise it went quiet, I waited only until it was light enough to see and quickly packed up. By then the sun was up, I began walking around looking for evidence of what had tormented me the night before. And right there in some soft sand were the tracks of the beast. Not just one set, but many sets. They were clearly dog tracks and some of them were pretty big, but not just one dog there were tracks from a whole pack of dogs!

Cliff overlooking Sugar Creek

Now I can't say for sure what Lily or Billy encountered while they were out at Sugar Creek, but I met a pack of wild dogs. And I am quite lucky because dogs are not scared of humans and once they've gone wild they tend to get mean and can be pretty dangerous. So if you are out in the Sugar Creek area be careful because there are wild dogs out there, and maybe a werewolf too.

Psalm 139:7-12

"Where can I go from your Spirit? Where can I flee from your presence? If I go up to the heavens, you are there; if I make my bed in the depths, you are there. If I rise on the wings of the dawn, if I settle on the far side of the sea, even there your hand will guide me, your right hand will hold me fast. If I say, 'Surely the darkness will hide me and the light become night around me', even the darkness will not be dark to you; the night will shine like the day, for darkness is as light to you."

God knows where each and every one of us is at and what we are doing, remember that His loving hands of protection are on each one of His children.

Urban Legends of Lincoln County Missouri

16

CHARLIE LINAHAN

Almost everyone in Lincoln County has heard of the Paw Paw House. Now if you haven't it sits on the west side of Cuivre River State Park on Frenchman's Bluff Road. There is nothing left of the house anymore, except for the chimney which just stands alone overlooking the Cuivre River valley where a man named Charlie Linahan used to hunt and fish. It is a sad reminder of the good old days when things were much more simple and life made more sense. This story is not about the Paw Paw House but rather about the man that built the Paw Paw House.

Well I had several stories told to me about old Charlie Linahan, so I'd like to play a little game with you! It's called 'fact or fiction; you decide'.

Story number one. Fact or fiction? It's your call.

It all started as I was sitting alone at my house one rainy Friday night just watching some TV when the phone rang. I wondered who on earth would be calling me this late at night. When I answered the phone the voice that greeted me was that of a man who sounded as if he had been haunted by some dark truth for a very long time. He told me that he had been holding on to this secret for many decades and felt that this was finally the time for him to tell somebody, but he didn't want his name mentioned so we will just call him John.

He started into his tale by asking me if I had heard of the Paw Paw House. When I said that I had he continued. "I have to tell you that the man who built the Paw Paw House, Charlie Linahan, did not die from natural causes." I listened closely as John spoke. "Charlie was murdered by the sons of the men in the Good Old Boys Club."

Now anyone should know that if you mention murder to a reporter that it is certainly going to pique their curiosity. "Do you know who did it?" I asked him

John told me a little more about this club. He told me that The Good Old Boys Club was created some time between the 1920's to the 1970's. They would have their meetings at a place called 'The Lonely Heart Club', it was a men only club along the bank of the Cuivre River down by

Frenchman's Bluff Road. Only the well-to-do men from Lincoln County were ever allowed to be a part of the Good Old Boy's Club. Their members included a State Representative, a Mayor for Troy, a Sheriff, even a city Marshall, it was basically made up of any high class men from Lincoln County. He went on to tell me that if there was ever a man, or one of their children, in the club that did wrong then those other men within the club would make certain that it got swept under the rug.

Finally he answered my question "Yes I do, but I want to give you a couple of phone numbers for people who know more about it than I do. But let me tell you what I know. You see now Charlie had thousands of dollars or more worth of Native American artifacts on display in his house. Well a few sons of those Good Old Boys decided that were gonna head on over to Charlie's and take those artifacts. They had decided that they would just go on in there rough him up and take his stuff. These boys put on masks and headed into his house where they beat up the 85 year old man and tied him to a chair. Then they went and loaded up the trunk of their car with his things. Then came back another time, but this last time they burnt up that house with Charlie alive inside it."

"But that's not the end of the story. The Sheriff being in the club, he just went and swept it aside saying that Charlie had committed suicide. That somehow the old man had just burned up his own house while he was in it." John had finished his story and then gave me two phone numbers to call. He said that if I called them that it would prove everything that he said was true.

Fact or fiction?

I called the first number and found that it was an older farmer that still lived in the community. Back many years ago he had been a State Representative. I made an appointment to come over and talk to him.

When I arrived the sun was shining brightly, but there was a chill in the air. He had a flea market going on, but no one was there other than me. I had been looking around a little bit when I heard a golf cart coming through the field from a big white house. As he pulled up I handed him my card.

"You Norm?" He asked me. I nodded yes, but didn't speak a word. "I've been reading and saving your articles. You do good work."

We talked for a while and I could tell that he was a very intelligent man who certainly knows his local history. But this man also did not want his name mentioned so from here on out we'll just call him Billy.

Billy told me that old Charlie Linahan kept all these artifacts in his house and loved to show them to everybody. It didn't matter who you were he was happy to invite you inside and let you have a look. But there were three teenage boys who got the smart idea that they were going to steal the artifacts and take them to St. Louis and sell them. So they went into Charlie's house late one night, tied up the old man then went on to fill up their car before they lit a fire and took off.

According to Billy there was a Boy Scout troop camping just down the road who saw the smoke from the fire. The Boy Scouts rushed down to the house and were able to get Charlie out just in time. But poor Charlie was never the same after the fire and about two weeks later committed suicide.

Billy seemed very sincere as he spoke to me, but you just cannot stop a reporter from digging.

Fact or fiction?

I called the last number that John had given me wondering if it was going to be a snake in the grass. The phone rang several times before it was answered by an older woman. I scheduled a time to come by her house and talk. I pulled up in front of a two story Victorian home in Troy. As I got out of my car a sudden cold chill overtook me. I knocked on the door and a sweet looking older lady opened it. She had snow white hair and the deepest blue eyes I had ever seen, as she invited me in it was as those blue eyes stared right down into my very soul. I stepped inside and the screen door let out a terrible squeak that made me jump. She turned with her walker and led me into the living room where I sat by a big fireplace. Then she offered to get me some tea and headed back out of the room.

I sat there waiting as every part of my body felt like it was being pricked by pins and needles. The whole house felt evil I knew that there were bad spirits there, I couldn't see them but I could certainly feel them. As she returned with the tea I caught the faint smell of something sweet cooking. She poured my tea and sat down.

I got straight to the point. "What can you tell me about Charlie Linahan?" I asked her.

"Well let me see. Now that would have been around 1967! Charlie was such a good man, he would have done anything to help out anyone." I watched as a tear came up in her blue eyes and she wiped it away. As she told me about him her voice was like a nightingale singing. She told me that he used to run the drug store in town, and

83

that if you didn't have the money that he would always make a way so that you could get the medicine that you needed.

"He was just such a good man." Her voice cracked and I could tell that she knew more than she was telling me. "It was such a shame what happened to him." She turned away from me trying to keep me from seeing her cry.

"He just didn't deserve that, and then they just went and swept it under the rug. Those three teenagers killed him, we all knew it. The Sheriff, the medical examiner, they knew it but just went right on and ruled it as if he had died of natural causes. And they covered it all up even though everyone in town knew what really happened." She stood up and I knew that she had told me all that she was going to, even though I could tell that there was more to the story that she wasn't telling me. "But since it was a murder could you please not give anyone my name?"

I agreed as she led me back to the door. As I stepped out onto the front porch the cold chill that I had since arriving there left me. In my opinion as a Minister, her house was full of evil spirits. I'm thinking about giving her a call and seeing if she would like for me to come out and bless her house and run all those spirits right out of it.

Fact or fiction?

After these two interviews I decided to do a little digging of my own. I happened to find none other than Charlie Linahan's own grandson, Colin C. Campbell. He was more than happy to talk with me. He shared some pictures, personal stories of the good times that they'd had together and even the truth about old Charlie Linahan's death.

He told me that his Grandfather had owned the first drug store in Troy, Mo, and had a house built on Cap Au Gris Street, but he didn't remember the year. He said that his Paw Paw had needed some place to go to hunt and fish, so he and two of his buddies got together sometime in the 20's or 30's and built a little two room log cabin on the lower part of the Cuivre River on the East bank. They used it for hunting and fishing or even just as a little getaway lodge. But the cabin kept getting flooded so they moved it up on the hill to where the old chimney now stands.

"Now after Grandma died Paw Paw just wasn't the same, he could not live in the big house on Cap Au Gris anymore. So in 1938 Paw Paw sold his drug store and his big house and moved into his cabin. But I have to tell you that the plaque that the park put there is wrong. It was never called The Paw Paw House because of the trees, it was called the Paw Paw House because I called it my Paw Paw's house."

"My Grandpa used to work as a maintenance man at Camp Sherwood Forest within the park. But when he got real sick he had to stop working, but the park rangers would come by every day and check up on him. They would stop in and see if he was doing alright or if maybe he needed something from town. But one day when the ranger came by he didn't get an answer. He knocked a few more times before he let himself in knowing that my Grandfather always left the door unlocked. And there he was laying dead on the kitchen floor."

"The coroner did the autopsy and ruled that he had died from stomach cancer. This was in 1964 when he was

85 years old. We had no further questions because we knew that he had been suffering from the cancer for the last two years before his death."

"Before you go I would like to tell you a story about my Paw Paw. I remember one time when we all lived in the big house on Cap Au Gris, when we had to run out to the store for something. My Mother had left the water on in the bathtub upstairs and when we came back it had flooded the whole house.

Well my Grandma was as mad as a wet hornet, but Paw Paw hugged her tight and told her not to worry about the material stuff, that it could all be replaced and made her smile. My Paw Paw he loved his life and he lived a good full life. May God rest your soul, I love you.

Proverbs 12:17-19

"He that speaketh truth sheweth forth righteousness: but a false witness deceit. There is that speaketh like the piercings of a sword: but the tongue of the wise is health. The lips of truth shall be established for ever: but a lying tongue is but for a moment."

17

IS MISS FANNY A MURDERER?

In the year 1834 a man by the name of William Florence settled on a little piece of land in Lincoln County, just West of Auburn, Missouri. He brought his wife and two boys. Thomas was the oldest who was around nine and the younger boy was named William. William Florence ran a small horsepower grain mill. It had been raining for several days, but on this late summer day in 1838 it was bright and sunny with a light breeze. Mr. Florence needed a few supplies, so he left his mill in the hands of Aaron, his slave, and headed into town. William was gone for several hours and on his returned to discover that his wife had let the boys next door to their neighbor's orchard to get some peaches.

Mr Florence was mad because he knew their neighbor William C. Prewitt had a mean old slave lady named Fanny. And she had more than once threatened to do bodily harm to the boys if she caught them over in the orchard.

With fear in his heart William Florence ran for the orchard. All the while he prayed to God to keep any harm from coming to his boys. He searched the orchard and found no sign of his sons. He then headed to the Prewitt's house to confront Fanny one-on-one. She was out in the yard hanging clothes on the line. He walked straight over to her and told her that if she caused any harm to his boys that she would pay. She denied even having seen them.

There was nothing that Mr. Florence could do, so he headed back home. Once he got there he sent Aaron to go to all the neighbors and then into town and tell everyone that his boys were missing. Aaron headed out on the fastest horse that they owned, while Mr. Florence continued to search until it was too dark to see. He was up before the dawn to start searching again the next morning. To Mr. Florence's surprise when he stepped outside there were about a hundred men waiting to search with him. These men included Sheriff Sitton, a member of the state legislature, Hans Smith (a brilliant orator of that day) even a surveyor named Burton Palmer among many other local folks.

The search continued for two full days until Burton Palmer saw some turkey buzzards flying in low lazy circles. He followed them straight to the children's bodies. They were laying in the creekbed weighted down with stones. It appeared that they had been put there when the creek had been high from the rains and then exposed as the water level dropped. Sadly the evidence was there on the exposed flesh that the buzzards had already gotten to work on the boys.

That evening Sheriff Sitton arrested Fanny, her husband Ben and their son Elick. The interrogation for Elick was brutal, with the questioners pulling the boy into the woods by a rope around his neck. Elick confessed that his mother had told him about how she hit the boys with a horse yoke and then threw them into a sinkhole in the creek, but he had no other information. The prisoners were then taken in for a preliminary trail where their son was released, but Fanny and Ben were to remain in jail awaiting a jury trial.

At this time Mr. Prewitt Fanny and Ben's owner returned from Philadelphia. Upon hearing what had happened he immediately began preparing a defense for his two slaves. The trial started on the first Monday in November of 1838. Upon Elick's testimony the dismissed all charges brought against Ben. After Ben was let go Mr. Prewitt appealed for a change of venue, he did not believe that Fanny could get a fair trial in Lincoln County. The appeal was granted and the trial was moved to Warren County for April of 1839. Meanwhile Fanny was sent to the Pike County jail for safe keeping as many people feared that she would be lynched.

Fanny's trial held held at the Warren County Courthouse in Warrenton, Missouri. It took almost no time for her to be found guilty of murder in the first degree and sentenced to death by hanging. After the sentencing Elick came forward and swore that his confession was a lie and that he had only said it because he was in fear for his life, and had been forced to say it while being tortured. With Elick's statement the case was appealed to the Supreme Court. In October of 1839 the Supreme Court overturned the lower court's ruling stating that Warren County could not sentence her because it had no jurisdiction over the case. Also because a slave owner was not entitled to change the venue for a slave. The case was then sent back to trial in Lincoln County, but now Fanny's son's confession was no longer admissible.

With the lack of evidence the case quickly fell apart as there was no evidence to convict her on. Fanny was acquitted. The people of Lincoln County were outraged. And two young boys died without justice. To this day no one has been found guilty in the murders of William and Thomas Florence.

Hebrews 4: 13

"Nothing in all creation is hidden from God's sight. Everything is uncovered and laid bare before the eyes of Him to whom we must give account."

18

SANDY CREEK RAN RED

Let me take you back, if you will, to the year 1804, to the homestead of William McHugh. This was the day that Sandy Creek ran red. It was a day much like any other, only this day a few of Mr. McHugh's horses had gotten loose, so he called on his three boys to go fetch them. The boys James the oldest, William Jr. the middle and Jesse the youngest, headed up the creek looking for the horses. I'm sure that if they had known what waited for them that day they would have stayed home. James followed the tracks, glad to know that they would be riding back home. About an hour after they left home they finally found the horses. The boys had only started back to their home when they met a friend, a man they all knew who was supposed to be a great Indian scout, Frederick Dixon (though I might doubt that he was that great at scouting).

The two older boys kept on their horses and told Jesse that he could ride with Mr. Dixon, because he was youngest and smallest. They hadn't rode long before the horses wanted to stop and drink. As they were stopped along the bank of Sandy Creek arrows began to fly around them. At least one Indian was concealed behind some large sycamore trees on the opposite bank. The two older boys were killed immediately and fell into the creek, their blood mixing into the water.

The Indians let out a crazed war cry, the horse that Jesse and Mr. Dixon were on spooked and threw the two to the ground. They jumped to their feet as fast as they could, but Mr. Dixon was much faster than the young boy. And though Jesse was just a young boy and MR. Frederick Dixon was supposed to be a brave Indian scout, he ran on leaving the boy far behind him. Even when the boy cried out for him to not leave he did anyways, to fearful for his own life to even think upon the child.

It was only moments before the Indians were caught up to Jesse McHugh, and even as the Indians tortured him Mr. Dixon kept on running.

I sure would like to have been a fly on the wall of that house when Mr. Dixon got the and told William McHugh what had happened. I don't imagine it could have been the truth because if it had been Mr. McHugh probably would have picked up his gun shot him right where he stood.

The three boys were each wrapped in a sheet and buried in the same grave on the North side of Sandy Creek. Their name were carved into a big oak tree by their grave. They were laid to rest like young guards forever watching over the creek to see that such a terrible thing never happens there again. It was said that the killing was retribution for Mr. McHugh having killed three of the tribal dogs.

As a good reporter should, I went out to Sandy Creek as close to where the massacre happened as I could get. I could feel the unrest in the area it was as if every breeze through the trees carried young Jesse's voice crying out not to be left behind. Though the water of Sandy Creek washed the blood downstream you can still feel the presence of what happened in this place. In my mind I could hear the war cries of the Indians and sweet Jesse begging for mercy.

John 15:13

"Greater love has no one than this: to lay down one's life for one's friends."

Urban Legends of Lincoln County Missouri

19

CHARLES SCHROEDER

I thought that for once I would write about some blue collar people. Now you have probably never heard of these people, but after this story you are sure to appreciate this family's dedication to building our great country. They are a family that truly made Lincoln County. No, they were not politicians, neither were they rich. This was a family that went out and worked hard to make a living and to make Lincoln County great. These were the type of people that I would call my friends. Sadly, I don't have the time to tell you about the whole family, so I will just pick one in particular.

His name was Charles August Schroeder and he was born in Mansfield, Germany on August 3rd, 1845. At the age of five Charles came with his parents to America where they settled on a farm in southern Lincoln County, just north of Wright City. When Charles turned 18 he left home and served as a volunteer on the Union side of the Civil War.

After serving his country he came home, where he met his bride, Kathleen Weiszbrod. They were wedded on March 10th,1875, and made their home on the family farm near Big Creek in Lincoln County. It was in this time that Charles had begun to work at his father's saw mill that sat along the banks of Big Creek and Coon Creek. In 1876 their father sold the mill to his two sons. Charles and Kathleen had only a few short years together before she passed away on July 20th of 1878. On January 26th of 1878 Charles was united in marriage with Julia Weiszbrod. This proved to be a lasting marriage as they had nearly 53 years together and had ten children.

In 1886 Charles bought his brother's half of the mill out-right from him, which he ran until the day it closed in 1904.

Charles August Schroeder may have been born across the world in Mansfield, Germany, but he died here in Lincoln County, Missouri. And I salute him for the contributions the he made for this country and for this county. You worked hard and brought your living home by the sweat of your brow and the blisters on your fingers. Thank you, sir, for the lumber that built many of the homes we see in this area today. You are truly a hero, God Bless the Schroeder family and the work that they did to help build our wonderful county.

Genesis 3:19
"By the sweat of your brow you will eat your food until you return to the ground, since from it you were taken; for dust you are and to dust you will return."

20

LINCOLN COUNTY MOMO

The night is dark and the moon is hidden by the clouds, as you go for your evening walk along the riverside. When you are suddenly overcome by the wretched odor much like rotten eggs, a sound like leaves crunching underfoot causes you to turn. But there is nothing there. A chill runs up and down your spine as your hair stands on end, behind you a twig snaps. You spin around and are face to face with the legendary Momo Monster. It's huge hairy body looms over you, and it's bright orange eyes shine in the dim moonlight, as you fear that you may be taking your last breath.

Don't go out at night or he will come for you!

Momo is the local legend similar to the Bigfoot of the Pacific Northwest. He was so popular back in the seventies that they wrote a song about him and even made a low budget horror movie called 'Momo the Missouri Monster'. I tracked down the movie to watch it, it wasn't easy as it never had a large public release. I didn't understand why until I watched it. It may have stunk worse than the actual monster himself. There have also been a few books written on the subject and even several documentaries (one of which I actually managed to sit down and watch the entire production).

Momo is reported to have a large pumpkin shaped head with a furry body. He has long black hair that looks like a shaggy rug which hangs down and covers his eyes. He is said to stand around seven feet tall, and to have a terrible musky odor. The first public report was made in 1971 near Louisiana, Missouri. That report was made by two ladies named Joan and Mary. It is said that Momo liked the Mississippi River because all the reports at that time came from right along the river.

The most well known report of Momo took place in the afternoon of July 11th 1972. It was a hot afternoon with a slow warm wind. Eight year old Terry and his five year old brother Wally were playing in their backyard at the foot of Marzolf Hill on the outskirts of Louisiana, Missouri. Their older sister Doris was inside the house when she heard her brothers screaming. She looked out the bathroom window and was shocked and horrified by what she saw.

There was a huge black hairy man-like creature standing by a tree, his huge hands clutching the bloody corpse of a dog. The creature was at least seven feet tall and it's head sat right on it's shoulders, like it didn't have a neck at all. It's head was big and round like a pumpkin, and out from behind it's shaggy black hair were two brightly glowing orange eyes.

What the children described that day has painted an image in our minds as to what we will always picture as Momo The Missouri Monster.

But I am sure you are asking yourself, 'Louisiana is in Pike County, What does this have to do with Lincoln County?'

Let me tell you. On June 30th 1972, not even a full month before the children's sighting there was a sighting right here in Lincoln County. Two young men from Troy were out at a secluded area of the Cuivre River. These two men named Tim and Vaughn had spent the day fishing from a high bank that overlooked a lower bank on the opposite side of the river. As Vaughn stood to take a break the two notice an awful smell in the air. Vaughn looked around and saw what he thought was a naked hairy hippie walking along the opposite side of the river.

Vaughn hollered at Tim to look at the Hippie who he figured must have been on some of that wacky tobacco. Tim jumped up and looked, but he knew it wasn't a hippie.

The creature was much taller than a normal man and was covered with hair all over. And it too looked as if it's head sat right on it's shoulders. Both men tried to come down the bank to get a better look, but the creature turned and charged right for them causing the men to panic and flee for their lives.

It was July of 1972 when a second report comes from a man and woman from West Virginia, who were passing through Missouri. They had stopped at Logan Conservation Area in northern Lincoln County to stretch their legs. When they left their vehicle they smelled something that smelled like an entire family of skunks. When they looked around they saw him standing there, his big pumpkin head and glowing candle eyes let them know who he was. He was nearly seven feet tall and had to weigh four-hundred pounds. He ran for them and they ran straight for their car.

They barely made it inside when he reached it and shook their car and tormented them for thirty minutes before finally tiring of them and disappearing back into the woods from which he had come.

Whether you are in the Pike County hills or the Lincoln County forests, there are some spooky stories around these parts. And back before the Momo and Bigfoot stories there were plenty of stories of lights in the sky. Either way 'Don't go out into the night' is what they would tell you!

Isaiah 56:9

"Come, all you beasts of the field, come and devour, all you beasts of the forest!"

Ezekiel 34:25

"I will make with them a covenant of peace and banish wild beasts from the land, so that they may dwell securely in the wilderness and sleep in the woods.

21

DAVID L. KESSLER

Who is the man named David L. Kessler? Off of State Highway KK about 5 miles north of Troy, Missouri there is a state conservation area in his memory. Who was he to have an entire conservation area named for him and where did he come from? Where was he born and how did he die? Well, let's get down to it then.

David L. Kessler was born August 10th in the year 1911 in Dardenne, Missouri to a middle-class family. His father, Leonard John Kessler, was born in 1883 and died in 1975. David's mother, Bettie Stevenson-Kessler was born in 1885 and died in 1968. He had three sisters an older on named Connie and two younger sisters named Ruby and Lillian.

While they had a good life in St. Charles County, David's dad had always wanted to be a farmer. Then the day came when Leonard Kessler found his dream. His excitement was much more than David's who didn't want to leave his friends in the city. But Leonard Kessler had found property north of Troy it was just over a hundred and fifty acres with about two-thirds fields and the rest wooded. He was happy that they would be able to build a house and have plenty to hunt and eat from the woods. SO the family packed up and headed to Lincoln County.

The family quickly adjusted to their new life and David learned from his Dad how to farm. When David turned 18 he married his lovely wife Lorene, they lived together on the farm until she passed away in 1963. David took the death of his wife very hard. Then five years later when his mother died, in 1968 he told his kinfolk and friends that it seemed like his whole world was falling apart.

Soon after his mother's passing David hired a handyman to help around the house and farm, and to take care of his father, Leonard.

It seems like this is close to where the story would end, but this is truly where it begins! The mystery lies around the events of David's death and if there is anyone out there who knows the truth, then feel free to call me! From the many stories that I was told, the following is what I have pieced together.

In the year 1969 David and his hired hand went out to stretch some barbed wire on the fence that they were building, while David's dad decided to stay inside that day. The two men left around 6 in the morning, but David never returned. After a year of searching Leonard had his son declared dead and held a funeral for him in 1970.

I was also told that David's hired hand had accidentally slipped while they were stretching the barbed wire cutting David badly. Which then caused Mr. Kessler to go into a rage berating and cussing out the hired hand, before firing him. Which then caused the hired hand to grab a hammer and beat David to death, then dispose of his body by grinding it and feeding to the hogs. The hired hand immediately left Lincoln County never to be heard from or seen again. But this is just hearsay, but the question remains, as to the hired hand's disappearance too.Me, being the ever-questioning journalist, I wanted to know how much of this was truth, so I went looking for information on David Kessler's friends. I found an older man who knew David, so I asked him out right if what I had been told was true.

He looked at me while scratching his head, and told me that he didn't really recollect how it was that David died. My next question was how exactly did the state end up with his land? The older man knew this one. He told me that with David and Lorene never having had children, that they had made their wills out to give all their property to the state. At least that part of the mystery was solved. And now you too know the legend of David L. Kessler.

Matthew 6:19-21

"Do not lay up for yourselves treasures on earth, where moth and rust destroy and where thieves break in and steal, but lay up for yourselves treasures in heaven, where neither moth nor rust destroys and where thieves do not break in and steal. For where your treasure is, there your heart will be also."

22

MAJOR JAMES WILSON

It was a war unlike any seen before, and hopefully will never be seen again. It was a war that pit brother against brother, and father against son. It split the United States in half and many tears were shed on the battlefield. But a crime against humanity was being done, and so it was that the war had to be fought. It was the war against slavery. Every human is created equal, no matter what color their skin is, or if they are male or female. Everyone has the right to be free! I'm sure you know that I have been talking about the Civil War, it began April 12th 1861 and ended May 9th 1865. The first shots rang out at Fort Sumter, South Carolina on April 12th 1861 and the first battle outside of Manassas, Virginia July 21, 1861.

It was mostly north against south with a few split states, Missouri was one of these split states, though mostly Confederate. Union troops occupied a little town in the northeastern part of the state called Troy, early in the Civil War. In 1861 the Federal Army set up camp at Spring Park using the Methodist Church as their headquarters, and Troy came to be used as a Union recruitment station throughout the war.

Confederate Colonel Timothy Reeve was a Baptist Minister who formed a guerrilla unit in Southeast Missouri as the Civil War was beginning. Reeves was from Ripley

County on the Arkansas border. His unit later became part of the 15th Missouri Calvary Regiment. Reeve and his soldiers were often found fighting against the Union Militias that were headed by Major James Wilson, a native of Troy. Many of these battles were standard Missouri guerrilla style warfare. Reeves had never forgiven Wilson for a surprise attack on Christmas Day on the Reeves camp near Doniphan, Missouri.

Confederate General Sterling Price invaded Missouri in 1864. Major James Wilson and a large number of soldiers were captured at the battle of Pilot Knob, Missouri on September 27th 1864. The Confederates had spread out from Pilot Knob to an area just East of current day Highway 185. On the morning of August 3rd, 1864 a Confederate Colonel, who was also believed to be an Inspector General called the prisoners into formation, Major Wilson and five others were separated from the formation and put under watch of a double guard because they had been identified as having been militia members.

Instruction had been given to the Colonel of the Confederate regiment to wait with the prisoners until Colonel Timothy Reeve arrived to take command of the prisoners. When Colonel Reeve arrived he took the prisoners and led them into a wooded area near St. John's Creek and put them to death by firing squad. Their bodies were found three weeks later by a young man walking by the creek. A justice of the peace and a postmaster from the neighboring town of Beaufort were notified of the find. And a neighbor was finally able to identify the men by their personal effects. They then buried the bodies where they found them.

During these three weeks Colonel Amos Maupin had been searching for the missing men, he was notified of their discovery and went to examine the bodies himself. He had the bodies dug up and re-examined and then curiously re-buried them in the same place.And this is where our mystery begins, is with the final resting place of five Union soldiers. Several U.S. Military telegraphs have been found regarding this matter. The first telegram gave the order to recover the remains and then transport them to Washington, Missouri.

There, five of the remains were to be buried with Major Wilson's remains going on to St. Louis, Missouri. A return telegraph was sent back from Lieutenant J. D.

Jacoby from the Quartermaster's Corps to General Ewing stating that there was not enough time to remove all the remains and that he would only be sending Major Wilson's body to Washington.

Through other telegrams we learn that Major Wilson's remains indeed went to St. Louis where they waited in the courthouse until finally being sent home to Lincoln County, Missouri.

On August 2nd 1870 a monument was erected in his, and his men's, honor in the Troy city cemetery by the post of the Grand Army of the Republic. Major James Wilson fought for what he knew was right, even against all odds.

Upon learning that he had joined the war on the Union side his wife took their children and left him going back to her family in Virginia. Even his family including his brother broke all ties with him because of their Confederate sympathies. But still Major Wilson stood and fought! Major James Wilson was born May 3rd 1834 and died October 3rd 1864 at the age of 30, he is buried in the Troy city cemetery in Troy, Missouri.

I have lived in Lincoln County for 35 years and I have come to find that most of Lincoln County's residents stand up for what they think is right. I am proud to say that Major James Wilson is from Troy, Missouri and that is why I wrote this story.

Isaiah 56:1

"Thus saith the LORD, Keep ye judgment, and do justice: for my salvation is near to come, and my righteousness to be revealed."

Urban Legends of Lincoln County Missouri

23

THE CAT LADY

Halloween is creeping up on us and pretty soon ghosts, goblins and ghouls will be everywhere. And what is Halloween without a good scary story about cannibalism! So pour yourself another cup of coffee or cocoa, sit back in your lazy chair and read the legend of the cat lady.

The year is 1984 and in a little house just south of Moscow Mills lives Miss Molly. Now no one is quite sure exactly they way things were or how Miss Molly was feeling, but from those witnesses that knew her then we can piece together most of the tale of her final days.

Miss Molly liked to walk back and forth in her old kitchen, her walker scuffing along in front of her, she would often think on her life, how it had gotten so bad was beyond her. Just two years before her husband of fifty years had died, and now she was all alone. Not even on holidays would their grown children would stop by for a visit. She would sit at her kitchen table and look over her fifty or sixty cats. She was two days from turning eighty-five and knew that no one understood what it was like to be old, alone and forgotten. Even her nearest neighbors, who were probably a half-mile away, would keep their distance. If they were outside they might wave whenever Miss Molly would go to town once a week to get cat food.

The cats would meow and beg for their dinner, it took her practically her whole income check just to keep them fed, and that was why she had no heat in her house anymore. But still their company was better than no company at all. Every evening she would feed the fifty or sixty cats before fixing her own supper. She got the bag of food out and headed to the front room, talking to the cats the as she usually did.

I wonder if she thought about a saying she commonly said as the pain began to shoot through her arm and across her chest. She would say, "What you get for gettin' out of bed is just another day like every other day." The bag of cat food swung from her walker as she fell to the floor. Did she holler for help as she lay on the floor, did she cry out knowing that no one would hear her? How long did she lay there hoarse from yelling before the Lord decided to take her home?

How long after she had gone did the cats begin to get hungry? Fifty or sixty of them, waiting for their dinner. What could they do? Just like any other wild creature, once the survival instincts kick in they will do whatever they have to do to survive, even if it means resorting to eating people. The weeks passed and the days grew colder. The cats began to die, the cold weather kept the smell down.

How long was it before that neighbor a half-mile away noticed that Miss Molly's car hadn't gone by lately. There were no tracks in the packed snow which had not been shoveled from the drive. She didn't get far driving up to Molly's because of the deep snow, she got out and started walking. She hadn't got far before she could smell the decay from inside the house. She knocked on the door the only response was from the few cats that remained alive caterwauling inside like demons.

She didn't attempt to go inside, she just hurried home and called the Lincoln County Sheriff's Department. They arrived about an hour later, and got the same response when they knocked. The decision was made to knock the door down. It didn't take long before the door popped open, the few remaining cats fled the house and disappeared into the woods.

Miss Molly lay in the middle of the floor in the front room. Her body was so disfigured that several of the deputies had to run out of the room because of the sight. They later said that she looked so bad that no one would have recognized her. Dead cats were scattered around the room, most of them in pieces from the few living cats having eaten them to stay alive.

The house stood for a while longer and some people tried to clean it up, but no matter what the stink remained. They finally gave in and had the house tore down. To this day no other home has been built where Miss Molly's home once stood. It made me wonder as to why no one had built there. But they say that if you go by there late at night that you can still hear the cats howling and wailing in the dark, it's said to be a terrifying sound that will make chills run up and down your spine.

So if you drive by Miss Molly's old home site watch out for some of those cats might still be out there. And you know they say that once an animal gets a taste of human blood that it wants nothing else. I drove out there recently around midnight and I didn't hear anything. But the next day I did notice some deep scratches on my driver's door, I guess it could have happened when I fell asleep for an hour or so.

Happy Halloween to all you folks out there. And a word of warning, while you're out trick-or-treating watch out for cannibal cats! These legends have been passed down for generations so you choose whether to believe them or not.

James 1:27

"Religion that God our Father accepts as pure and faultless is this; to look after orphans and widows in their distress and to keep oneself from being polluted by the world."

24

THE DUNCAN MANSION

Silex, Missouri was started in the 1880's when the North Hannibal Railway was extended to the town for the purpose of transportation. The post office in Silex has been operation since 1882. Perched on a cliff, like a great eagle, overlooking the small town sits the Duncan Mansion. My purpose here is to untangle some of the myths and mysteries that surround the Duncan Mansion.

Let me tell you a little bit about the man who built the great house. His name was Jesse J. Duncan and he was born in another Lincoln County town to the Southwest of Silex, called Olney, in 1870. He later attended the University of Missouri in Columbia, and in his third year received an appointment to cadet.

After graduating in 1893 with a law degree from the University of Michigan, he came back to Missouri after his graduation and opened a law office in Troy, Missouri. On June 6th 1900 he married Nora Belle McAllister from Bowling Green, Missouri. They settled in Lincoln County and had two children. Jesse and Nora built what we now know as the Duncan Mansion.

I've had many calls and heard many rumors about the Duncan family and the Duncan Mansion, but they are mostly that, rumors only. Some say that the Duncan family was mob connected, or that they sold bootleg whiskey to the Irish mob, known as the Hogan Gang, out of St. Louis. There are also tales of money laundering operations, and even of a cat house being run out of the mansion!

The most compelling rumor, though, was the Hogan Gang connection. So I decided to look into it. The leader of the Hogan Gang was Edward 'Jelly Roll' Hogan. Hogan seemed to serve as a State Representative at the

same time as Duncan did, Hogan served for five terms and Duncan only served for one. So I dug deeper and found where the confusion was.

Jesse Duncan served as a State Representative from 1907 until 1911, but Edward Hogan wasn't elected State Representative until 1916, five years after Duncan had already served. And then again Jesse Duncan was a State Senator from 1917 to 1921, and Hogan didn't become a

Senator until 1940. The confusion is easy to understand, but they truly were not working together.

I followed up on a few more leads and most of those were nothing more than hearsay. In all my research the one thing that I did discover was that the Duncans were a hard-working All-American family. I would have been proud to call them my neighbors or friends. Families like theirs is what has made America great.

Jesse and Nora's son Captain Marion Joseph Duncan and their grandson William B Duncan were both at Pearl Harbor on December 7th 1941. They died as American heroes.

In short, when you think about the Duncan Mansion, think about it with pride. And when you think about the Duncan family, remember them as they lived, as real hard-working Americans, and how their boys died as heroes. I salute them!

Matthew 7:12

"So in everything, do to others what you would have them do to you, for this sums up the Law and the Prophets."

In other words, treat people the way that you would like to be treated, and speak of them how you would like to be spoken about.

25

THE PIG FARMER

The year is 1979 and out on Highway J in southern Lincoln County sits a little pig farm. Here on the pig farm, in a small house lives a farmer named Frank, his wife, Betty and their daughter. Their daughter met a young man from Troy named Benjamin. It wasn't long before the two were madly in love, and not much longer still before they were married. Tragically only a year after they had said their vows the young woman was killed in a head-on collision not far from her childhood home on Highway J.

Frank was devastated at the loss of his only child. It was as if when she went she took his will to live. He fell into a deep depression and let everything around him slip past, ignored. Now, Betty could take a lot of things, but being ignored was not one of them. She might let Frank slide on the farm, but she was an entirely different matter than a few pigs.

When Betty couldn't bring her husband around she began to look elsewhere for attention, and of all places she got it from her daughter's widower, Benjamin! As the time passed Betty and Benjamin became more and more involved with each other. And Frank either didn't notice or didn't care, he just continued to be more lost to the world every day.

How Betty wanted to get away from Frank, but she knew that she could not, he had all the money and she had nothing. So she and her lover came up with a plan. She would convince Frank that she was truly worried about him and that maybe getting away from home might do him some good and get his mind off his beloved daughter. Now it was Benjamin's turn. Benjamin told Frank that they were going to go to Las Vegas and do some gambling, and somehow he even managed to trick the distraught man into thinking that he would need to withdraw his entire savings from the bank to take with them. And then he sent Frank on his way to the bank.

When Frank came home there in his living room sat his wife and his son-in-law. Benjamin had a shotgun in his lap pointed at Frank. Betty came over and snatched the briefcase he held away from her husband knowing that it contained their entire life savings. Her lover came behind her as they led poor old Frank out to the barn where they had laid sheet plastic over everything they could reach. Frank was standing on the plastic, a look of confusion on his face when the gun fired and he drew his last breath.

After they killed Frank they spent the next week grinding him up and feeding him to the pigs. When two weeks had passed after his death they called the police and reported him missing, stating that he had never returned from Las Vegas.

Everything was looking good for the two as the police bought every word they said. That was for about the first year, but soon Betty began to tire of Benjamin too. Benjamin felt guilty about what they had done to Frank. He began to become agitated and say that he could not live in the farmhouse any longer, Frank's ghost was haunting the place and driving him mad. She was able to tolerate his crying for another year before deciding that she'd had enough, it was time for Benjamin to join Frank. Benjamin saw what was coming as she began to take him to the barn one day. Somehow he was able to wrestle the shotgun from her hands and turn it back on her.

When the police arrived Benjamin was beside himself. He told the whole tale to the detectives, the entire time Frank's ghost stood to the side watching him. They arrested Benjamin and a short while later he was sent to an institute for the criminally insane, where he spent the remainder of his life.

Maybe with Benjamin's passing Frank's soul was able to rest, but then again maybe the restless spirit of a lonely heartbroken pig farmer still walks the grounds of that little farm. Believe it or not the choice is yours, some legends are real and some are just that, legends.

Deuteronomy 32:35
"To me belongeth vengeance, and recompence; Their foot shall slide in due time: For the day of their calamity is at hand, And the things that shall come upon them make haste."

26

MUTILATED COWS

It seems to me that there is always something bizarre going on in the little town of Elsberry, in the Northeast corner of Lincoln County, MO. So to Elsberry we have gone again. This time it is April of 1978 and there have been some strange things going on in the sky and some butcher has been cutting up the cows in this little town. People have even been going as far as to pull out their lawn chairs and six packs while they sit around all night hoping to see a UFO.

Rumors around the town were of people having seen bright lights that would whirl around the sky and then zip from the East to the West and then back from the West to the East again. But that wasn't all. Farmers on four different farms claimed that they had cattle that were mutilated.

On April 1st of 1978 five head of cattle were found mutilated, one of the cows were from the farm of Forrest Gladney. That poor cow was missing its right eye, right ear and its udders. Other cows were missing their male and female organs, rectal tissue, internal organs and various other body parts. It looked almost as if the parts had been removed with surgical instruments. And even though the cattle had been cut up there was almost no blood at the scenes. Even stranger still was that the buzzards and even the flies wanted nothing to do with the corpses.

People from all over came out to quiet little Elsberry hoping to get a glimpse of the lights. On June 21st of that same year some reporters from the St. Louis Post Dispatch came to town, and they published the most incredible story about the happenings. Next thing, news channels from St. Louis had sent reporters out as well! Everyone just wanted to get a picture or some film footage of the lights.

A local woman told the news that she had seen a glowing childlike figure running across one of the fields shortly before the mutilated cows had been found. Many people wondered if someone wasn't smoking what they were growing, but all joking aside, this was serious and the locals were scared.

I wondered about this story, so I took to the internet and scoured the FBI's files on mutilated cattle cases. There were literally thousands of cases across the mid-west throughout the 1970's and even since then! The reports from other areas were practically identical to the ones from Elsberry. The FBI claims to still be investigating these cases. But they are not easy to investigate yourself, things I encountered made it clear that the government was involved and knows exactly who or what is responsible and why they would do such a thing! It seems to be just another government cover-up.

Micah 7:5-6
"Do not trust in a friend; Do not put your confidence in a companion; Guard the doors of your mouth From her who lies in your bosom. For son dishonors father, Daughter rises against her mother, Daughter-in-law against her mother-in-law; A man's enemies *are* the men of his own household."

27

THE HAUNTED RAILROAD TRACKS

I recently learned that there are unresting spirits in the town of Foley, Missouri. This little town in Northern Lincoln County was platted in 1879 and was named after Addison Foley, who was the original land owner where the town is located. Foley was incorporated as a town in 1880 and at the last census taking in 2010 the population was only 161 people.

Two weeks ago I received a phone call from a very distressed and concerned citizen of Foley. She insisted that she did not want her name used in this story so we will just call her Ms. Bell. She sounded so scared that I was becoming concerned for her well-being. I asked her what had happened, and she began her tale. Ms. Bell explained to me that she lives close to the railroad tracks and that she has even spoken to many of her neighbors about this and they all laugh at her and think that she is plain crazy.

Finally she began to explain her horror. It started around four years ago, shortly after she moved to the small town. "Every night around 6:30 it starts, first is the train whistle. It blows and blows getting louder. I even have gone outside so many times, but there is never a train, but that doesn't stop the sound blaring on as if the train is right there. And then right after is the screaming, a horrible chilling scream. It makes me freeze and shudder every time I hear it. But again, nothing to make the sound. Then just before 6:40 it stops. I even brought my neighbors and a couple friends over, but they don't hear anything at all. I have walked the tracks and never found anything. You are my last resort. If you can't find anything, then I guess I am crazy."

I told Ms. Bell not to worry and that I would certainly look into it and let her know what I find out. So I started digging and was surprised at what I discovered. I truly believe that Ms. Bell can feel unresting spirits from the past.

On October 5th 1883 a local man by the name of Samuel Bridgeman had just put in a hard day's work and was heading home. Samuel was a plasterer and was well known around the county and respected for being good at his trade. He was quite tired this day from having worked mush later than usual. He just wanted to get home pull off his shoes and rest, so when he realized that if he walked the railroad tracks rather than the road that it would make his walk quite a bit shorter, he went for it. It was right at 6:30 when the train whistle first blew at the man on the tracks, but he was just too tired to move fast enough. As he scrambled to get off the tracks he caught his foot and tripped. He landed with his feet over the rail and his body safely off the side. Before he had time to move the train was there cutting off both his feet as it rushed past. He lay there bleeding and screaming. His screams were heard by a neighbor lady who ran over to him, but there was nothing that she could do, she left him as she ran into town for help. They managed to get him to the doctor's, but sadly there was nothing that could be done for the man. He succumbed to his injuries a little over two hours later.

Samuel Bridgeman was only 39 when he met his fate at the train tracks that evening. Oddly though, the woman who ran out to help Samuel Bridgeman, was the exact same age at the time as the woman who called me. And her house sat in the exact same place.

I went to Foley, Missouri and walked the tracks where he was said to have been. I walked and prayed, sprinkling holy water as I went. Praying that Samuel and Ms. Bell could have some peace.

I received a phone call from Ms. Bell not that long ago. I could hear the relief in her voice as she spoke to me, she told me that she no longer hears the phantom train whistle or the disembodied screaming.

Matthew 12:43-45
"When an impure spirit comes out of a person, it goes through arid places seeking rest and does not find it. Then it says, 'I will return to the house I left.' When it arrives, it finds the house unoccupied, swept clean and put in order. Then it goes and takes with it seven other spirits more wicked than itself, and they go in and live there. And the final condition of that person is worse than the first."

Urban Legends of Lincoln County Missouri

28

BLACK HAWK SPRING

Not too far away, in the Northern part of Lincoln County, Missouri in the middle of the night the wind dances through the treetops like a guardian over the land below. Sometimes you can smell the scent of burning wood as if from a nearby campfire. Listen closely. Can you hear the Native American drums beating as the sing their war song?

It is a legend that I have heard since moving to this area some years ago. There is tell of a hidden spring not far removed from State Highway KK called Blackhawk Spring. Back in the early 1800's Chief Blackhawk would bring his braves to the spring where they would camp and hunt. At the first they would sing songs of the hunt, and to be blessed with plenty.

But then in 1812 all that would change. When the war broke out the Chief would still bring his men to the spring, but now their songs had turned to songs of war, and their dances to ones of battle rather than the hunt.

Legend tells the words of their song. 'First, this land was God's. Then it was our ancestors, and now it is ours. White eyes has come to take our land. And we are going to fight until the last warrior falls.' During the war many of Blackhawk's men did fall. Today the locals that live around the spring say that sometimes at night the warriors come back to their spring. They dance around the fire and beat their drums. To the spirits of the fallen warriors the war of 1812 still rages on. They died protecting their land and now in their afterlife Blackhawk's warriors still protect it.

It took me months to learn the true location of the spring, learn who the owners are and to get permission to camp there. Finally I had received permission on one condition, never to reveal the location to anyone under any circumstances.

It was a moonless night when I set up camp just a short walk from the spring. I did not build my own campfire because I wanted to find out if the tales of being able to smell the phantom's fire were true. As the night went on and nothing happened I grew tired. It was about eleven at night when I climbed into my tent and readied myself to go to sleep. I lay on the floor of my tent waiting and listening for over an hour.

I was just starting to drift off when the wind gusted so hard it almost picked me and my tent up off the ground! I listened as the wind shifted up to the treetops and ever so faintly was the smell of a wood campfire. I sat up and listened, there it was, the war drums beating in the distance! Suddenly coyotes joined in on the song and drowned out the sound of the drums. I unzipped my tent and stepped out. It was a few moments before the coyotes quieted down, and then nothing. Silence.

They say that the human mind is a truly powerful thing, and that our imaginations can cause us to see and hear any number of fantasies that aren't actually there. Were the things that I experienced my imagination or did the fallen warriors come back on this dark night to perform their war dance around the lost spring? You decide.

Job 7:9-10

"As the cloud is consumed and vanishes away: so he that goes down to the grave shall come up no more. He shall return no more to his house, neither shall his place know him any more."

NOTES

Stories previously released in the Lincoln County Journal by Norman McFadden. Special thanks to the Lincoln Count Journal, and all those who helped make this possible.

ABOUT THE AUTHOR

Norman McFadden is the Author of the
"Legends of Leeper holler" series. A licensed Minister and
former pro wrestler, Norman resides in Lincoln County,
Missouri, where he continues to write and do various
works in ministry. For more information about the Author,
visit Polstonhouse.com today!

Urban Legends of Lincoln County Missouri

Norman McFadden

AVAILABLE FROM POLSTONHOUSE.COM

Norman McFadden

AVAILABLE FROM POLSTONHOUSE.COM

Urban Legends of Lincoln County Missouri

Norman McFadden

AVAILABLE FROM POLSTONHOUSE.COM

145

Urban Legends of Lincoln County Missouri

Norman McFadden

AVAILABLE FROM POLSTONHOUSE.COM

Urban Legends of Lincoln County Missouri

Norman McFadden

AVAILABLE FROM POLSTONHOUSE.COM

Urban Legends of Lincoln County Missouri

Norman McFadden

AVAILABLE FROM POLSTONHOUSE.COM

Urban Legends of Lincoln County Missouri

Norman McFadden

AVAILABLE FROM POLSTONHOUSE.COM

Norman McFadden

AVAILABLE FROM POLSTONHOUSE.COM

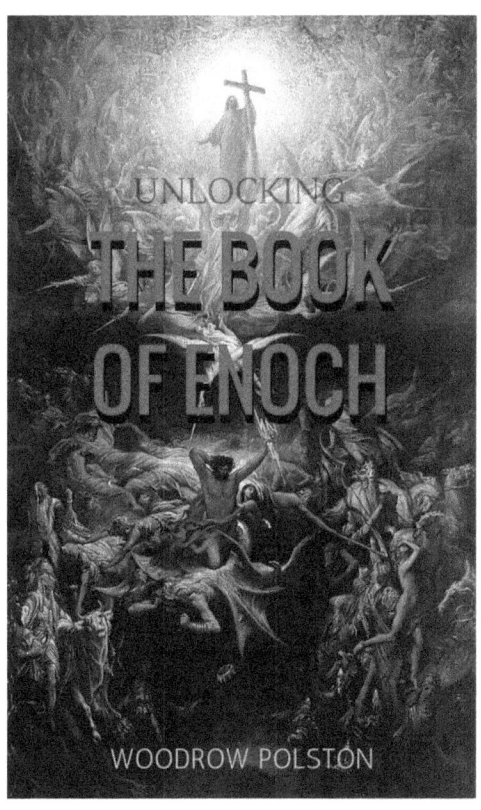

Urban Legends of Lincoln County Missouri

Norman McFadden

AVAILABLE FROM POLSTONHOUSE.COM

Norman McFadden

Urban Legends of Lincoln County Missouri